15/4/23

Tyso's Promise

TYSO'S PROMISE

Sally Robey

Ⓛ

Lutterworth Press
Cambridge

To Simon and Pru with love and thanks

Lutterworth Press
7 All Saints' Passage
Cambridge CB2 3LS

British Library Cataloguing in Publication Data
Robey, Sally
Tyso's promise
I. Title
823'.914[J] PZ7

ISBN 0-7188-2687-6

First published 1987 by Lutterworth Press

Typeset in Monophoto Plantin by
Vision Typesetting, Manchester

Printed and bound in Great Britain by
Redwood Burn Limited, Trowbridge, Wiltshire

1

Very cautiously, Tyso lifted the tarpaulin covering the back of the pick-up truck and peered out. His large dark eyes blinked at the glare of light that met him. The truck had pulled onto the large, well-lit forecourt of a transport cafe, and was dwarfed on every side by the bulk of huge container lorries resting on their journeys to and from the exciting places of the world. Such a journey was not for Tyso, though. All that he wanted to do was to put as many miles as possible between himself and Uncle Jo and Aunt Sarah, and without any delay. This had meant leaving behind Rosie, Edward and Gran, which had saddened him, the sorrow travelling with him as a heavy place somewhere inside his chest; however, it had to be.

In the months that had passed since his parents' deaths, he had continued to work for his uncle. The fear of leaving the young ones in his aunt's care had kept him at the site even though he suffered almost continually from his uncle's sharp tongue and heavy fist. The days were, however, no worse than the evenings when Tyso's job was to help him home from the pub and put him to bed.

If it hadn't been for Gran and her stories of the past, Tyso would have found these months unbearable. In the evenings, they would sit together by the yog* while Aunt Sarah watched television in the trailer. Rosie would crouch at Gran's feet and Edward would snuggle up on her lap whilst she talked of the days gone by. She told them of vardos†, brightly decorated and gleaming with brass, that wound their way through the country lanes, brilliant columns on their way to the gypsies annual meeting places, the great fairs of England. She spoke of the Herons, the Hernes, the Locks and many more who had lived in those spotless, horse-drawn

*fire   †caravans   1

homes. Especially, she spoke of the almost legendary Webster Boswell who had much learning and was admired by writers and scholars, and of his father, Tyso, who was killed by lightning in 1831.

"One day," Gran would say, poking at the yog with her foot, "one day you must go and see the tombstone. I've seen it. It's at Tetford, in Lincolnshire, you know." Tyso didn't know but he was very impressed and promised to go and look at it some time or other.

"Named for Tyso, you were," Gran went on, wagging a rheumatic finger at him. "Tyso Boswell."

Flames would flicker and another kick would send a cascade of sparks up into the black night. Gran would shift baby Edward slightly to ease the cramp in her legs and, as Rosie drew nearer to the comfort of the old skirt, Tyso would beg for a ghost story. Gran, like all gypsies, knew a number of these, and each one sent a thrill of fear through Tyso.

Those evenings had been good times. It almost made him homesick to remember them, and he had only left home that morning. He had not dared to tell anyone that he was going, not even Rosie, and he hated the idea of her waking up and finding him gone, but what could he do? Rosie was only a little girl. If he had told her, she might have let it slip by mistake. At least, like this, she wasn't involved and so couldn't be blamed in any way. After all, no need to drag her into it all. He was almost a man: she was a child. There would be no one left to protect her from Aunt Sarah, but he could take no more. The next time Uncle Jo had sworn at him or struck him, he would have hit back and he knew just how strong he was. After all, when he was out with his mates, wasn't he the one they relied on to get them out of trouble with the gaujo* boys when hurtling abuse grew too tame and it was time to turn to fighting. Under the tarpaulin, Tyso squirmed with the remembered pleasure of those encounters. It had been good to be in a group, sauntering along, confident; almost like an army, out against overwhelming odds. Yes, that had been something like life! But all that had ended with his mother's death. Since then he'd been trapped,

*non-gypsies

2

an orphan at the mercy of his aunt and uncle. That was how it felt, anyway.

Tyso had bundled together a shirt and another pair of jeans and taken five pounds from the green and gold jug on the shelf (he reckoned that Uncle Jo owed him that) and, moving very quietly, had managed to slip out without waking anyone. Several of the lurcher dogs that guarded the camp had growled threateningly, but as soon as he whispered to them they realised who he was and settled down to sleep. He looked back only once and that was for just long enough to promise that one day he would return for Rosie, Edward and Gran.

He had made his way south along the dual carriageway road, following it out of the town by keeping to the embankment. It was as the horizon began to glow with the first faint light of dawn that he spotted the pick-up truck in the lay-by below. Very carefully, he had slithered down the bank, clawing at the dead stalks of ragwort and other plants to stop himself from going too fast.

The driver was dozing, a half-eaten sandwich in his hand, and when he awoke a few minutes later, he had no idea that he had a passenger.

They travelled all day, only stopping for a short while around noon, and although Tyso longed to get out from his cramped position under the tarpaulin, he dared not do so because he could hear voices close at hand. He could only grit his teeth and endure as best he could the overpowering smell from the sacks of meal in the back of the truck. As he lay there, he went back in his mind over the past months, recalling how Uncle Jo and Aunt Sarah had constantly reminded him what a burden he, Rosie and Edward were, seeing to it that he worked every minute of the day helping with the scrap business in order to help pay their way. He remembered with anger how Aunt Sarah made Rosie go dukkerin'* with her, carrying a heavy basket of rubbishy lace and ribbons, or else kept her in the trailer cleaning. All of which was far too hard work for such a little girl to do. Then there was Edward, often tied to the steps to stop him wandering, and always dirty and underfed, crying from a seemingly endless stream of blows

*go out fortune-telling 　　　3

and abuse. No, somehow or other, it must be stopped. One day he would sort out Uncle Jo and Aunt Sarah, you see if he didn't!

At the end of that cold day in late winter, he climbed out of his hiding place to find himself among the flat unwelcoming fens of East Anglia. For mile upon mile they rolled, those remote sparsely inhabited acres, surging towards the distant, bleak marshes and the grey white-capped sea. They lay for miles without the shelter of a friendly wood or hospitable, hay filled barn. However, all this was hidden from Tyso as he stood stretching his aching limbs, hidden in the merciful night.

Voices close at hand caused him to duck down and scamper off between the high sides of the lorries, like a young cat exploring dustbins.

2

Once outside the circle of light the darkness rapidly swallowed him. For a gaujo that darkness would have been very daunting and almost impenetrable, but Tyso was a gypsy. For centuries his ancestors had lived by their wits and that had often meant turning night into day.

He stood listening. Behind him he could hear the murmur of voices and the muffled roar of engines being revved; in front of him was a wall of darkness. To his right was a roadway along which twinkled at intervals the headlamps of lorries and cars. Tyso didn't like roads, not that sort, anyway, and besides, he had had enough of travelling for one day. He wanted something to eat and somewhere to sleep, but he dared not go back to the transport cafe. People like him were seldom welcome.

He listened again. A few yards ahead of him he could hear the splash of water as it dripped from a land pipe into a dyke*. He took a few steps forward and stopped.

'Plop'. Somewhere near at hand a water rat had dropped into deep water. He sniffed and smelt the dank smell of mud and rotting plants. It was lucky that he had stopped for, now that his eyes were accustomed to the darkness, he could see below him the black sheen of slow moving water.

As he stood there uncertain what to do next, the moon drifted out from behind a cloud bank, bathing the countryside in an eerie light. The dyke stretched out in a straight line as far as the eye could see, the fields lying bare on either side of it, and, apart from an owl swooping low in search of food, there was nothing else. Or was there?

In the lee of the bank about a half a mile ahead there appeared to be a small clump of trees, which anywhere else would have passed without remark. Here, they stood out.

* a drainage canal with banks, or the banks themselves

Trees meant shelter and Tyso was only too aware of the cold east wind blowing into the fen lands all the way from Siberia. Trees would give him some shelter at least, and it wouldn't be the first time that he had gone hungry to bed. He set off along the dyke.

A short distance on, and the moon was again masked by cloud, but by this time he had got his bearings, although he needed to be very careful not to trip in a rabbit hole, or stumble over a stone, for the deep black water was waiting for him in the dark below.

After a while, he paused. Something was wrong. It wasn't the sound of the breeze stirring the dead sedge that bothered him, nor the uncanny feeling of being followed that affects most people who walk in lonely places at night. It was something ahead of him: something that should not have been there.

The clump of trees was less than three hundred metres away, and its shape loomed black against the darkness. But all was not well for from the depth of that blackness came a tiny yellow light.

Tyso stopped.

No sound.

Then he smelt the faint smell of wood smoke.

Someone had a fire. In all that loneliness, someone was at home.

You don't spend your life being moved on by the police, chased off by farmers and turned out by shopkeepers without learning to treat people cautiously. Tyso moved forward very slowly for a dozen metres and then dropped down and crawled for the rest of the way.

The smell of stew reminded him of how hungry he was. Then, he only just managed not to scream when, close at hand, a dog growled menacingly.

"Be quiet yer ol' fool," said a voice. "There 'baint anythin' there." The dog growled on. "Rest won't yer. There 'baint anythin' there – stands to reason, an' if there is, which there 'baint, it aint nothin' as you can do owt about. The witch stone is here an' me ol' crucifix. They'll be all the help we'll

6

need 'gainst what is out there, for, believe you me, it won't be 'uman, not out here tonight, it won't."

Not only could Tyso hear this strange monologue but he could also see in among the clump of trees, a tent, a very oddly shaped affair. It was bowed over like the top of a covered waggon in an American western film. He'd never seen a tent like this before but he knew that it was called a bender tent, a tent made by bending boughs over and covering them with a tarpaulin.

The dog had stopped growling but continued to whine in a nervous way, expressing its distrust of whatever was beyond the faint circle of light.

For several minutes nothing happened, and then Tyso's foot began to go to sleep and as he moved it, very carefully, he rustled some dead grass. It was a tiny sound but the response was immediate.

"Don' yer come a step nearer, do yer hear?" a voice wheezed out of the night and, lit by the fire's glow, there was a strange figure in what appeared to be a series of coats, each shorter than the last, giving a layered effect, and the top coat being tied with a hefty leather belt. Below the coats the trousered legs were thrust into a pair of short wellington boots, whilst on his head the man had a black felt hat pulled well down over his ears. Grey knitted gloves covered his hands which held, levelled straight at Tyso's waist, a business-like looking gun. "Go away. You're trespassin'," wheezed the voice. "Go away or I'll fill yer so full of lead you'll run blood like a fountain."

It wasn't courage so much as desperation that made Tyso hold his ground. The wind had grown more fretful and large drops of rain were stinging his face. Hunger gnawed at his stomach and the cold at his hands.

"I didn't know I was trespassing," he said, sounding, he hoped, far braver than he felt. "I was walking this way and saw your fire, right. So I made for it. That's all. Couldn't I come and warm myself for a bit? I'm awfully cold."

"How do I know that yer tellin' the truth? Yer might be the biggest liar since the Serpent in the Garden of Eden for all I

7

can tell. Yer might have half a dozen lads from the village with yer and I none the wiser. Or mebbe yer the man from the Council in disguise, or that silly bit girl from the Social." The voice creaked on but the hands holding the gun never waivered.

Tyso had had enough. He'd been called a liar, well fair enough, it wasn't the first time, and, anyway, lying could be very smart, like gold embroidery on a waistcoat. No, what got to him, what made him flush with anger and step forward into the circle of light, was to be called a man from the Council.

"Now look here," he shouted, fist raised, "stop talking and acting daft. Do I look like a man from the Council? Do I? Or a woman from the Social for that matter?" He almost choked he was so angry.

There was a pause, and then the gun was lowered.

"Yer only a lad," the old man muttered, trying by the disdain in his voice to cover the foolishness that he now felt. "Yer look near perished and starved. Set down an' warm yerself and, mebbe I can find yer some stew."

Tyso hoped that the old man could not see that he was shaking; of course, it was only because he was so cold, but nonetheless it wouldn't do for it to be noticed. He sat down on an upturned bucket and warmed his hands at the fire. A few minutes later a bowl of rabbit stew was put into his hands. He ate greedily.

"Good?" asked his host. Tyso nodded, wiping his mouth with the back of his hand in a way that always infuriated Aunt Sarah. "Ol' dog caught it. Rare rabbiter, ol' dog."

Silence.

Beyond the trees the rain was pouring down over the fields, but only a little of it found its way through the meshed branches overhead to spatter onto the fire. A lantern flickered at the entrance to the bender tent showing that it held no more than a pile of straw and blankets for a bed, and a few boxes piled with old saucepans and chipped crockery. However, the hard earthen floor was dry and there was not a scrap of rubbish to be seen.

The old man who had been sitting on a tea chest beside

Tyso got unsteadily to his feet and went into the tent to emerge a couple of minutes later with a transistor radio.

"The News. Must find out what's going on in the world."

They sat listening. The smooth accent of the newscaster seemed somehow as remote as if it came from another planet.

Tyso was in fact far too tired to care about doings in America and Russia; actually, he wasn't altogether too clear about where they were, although he knew that they were both very important for some reason or other.

"The rivers Nene and Ouse have risen to unprecedented levels for this time of year, and flood warnings have been issued over a wide area." The voice droned on as Tyso's head drooped on to his chest. He might have toppled forward into the fire had not the old man seized hold of him.

"Hold up, young'un. The right place for that is in the tent," he said. Tyso was far too tired to notice how weak the voice had become or the great effort that it took for the old man to steady himself as he got up. "Take yersel' in. I'll bank up the fire an' we'll sleep."

As Tyso, well covered by blankets, faded off to sleep on a pile of straw, he could see through the entrance to the bender tent the glowing embers of the fire. This was definitely the life. No more trailers for him. One day he would have a vardo, and roam the lanes of England like his great, great, he didn't rightly recall how many times great, grandfather before him. Tyso Boswell, he'd show them. He'd be his own man.

3

When Tyso woke the day was already several hours old. The fire was out and outside a curtain of rain hid the fields. Everything beyond the bender tent was sodden and miserable, though inside it was warm and reasonably dry.

At first when he peered out from under his pile of blankets Tyso could see no sign of the old man, then a wheezing cough made him look over towards a heap of bedding topped with a couple of tattered coats. The black felt hat rested where the pillow would have been in a normal bed and beneath it the pinched features were just visible, the eyes sunken behind the high cheek bones, the hawk nose, blade thin, dividing the pallid hollows of his face. The coverings scarcely moved so shallow was the breathing beneath them.

Tyso did not know what to do. It was a delicate situation. Should he go over with a cheery, "Good morning," or should he sneak out and try to light the sodden fire? The decision was made for him. As he clambered out of his bed, a faint whisper told him that the old man was awake.

"That you, boy?"

"Yes."

"Make a can of tea, there's a good lad. I'll tell yer . . ." but a fit of coughing interrupted the speaker and by the time it was over he was too weak to talk.

Tyso looked miserably at the soaked firewood. He found some matches and some paper, but it was no good. The paper browned and was eaten into a curve by the match, and then fizzled out. He went into the bender tent to ask what he should do. Did the old man have any paraffin? No answer. He shifted things about until he found a rusty can with a drop of pink liquid in the bottom. Taking a piece of rag he tore it, plaited it and soaked it in the paraffin. It worked at once, and

10

Tyso couldn't help but feel pleased with himself. Next he found the kettle with water still in it and this he put on to boil whilst he searched afresh, this time for the tea. It was in a tin painted with red roses, the only cheerful thing to be seen. In a far corner he found a battered tin teapot, and was just about to put the tea into it when a muffled noise from the bed stopped him. He went over. The old man lay there his eyes staring at the pot in Tyso's hand. He gave an almost imperceptible shake of his head.

"Not this pot?" Tyso asked. Again the tiny movement. Tyso shrugged. "I'll make it in the kettle." He went to put the teapot back where he had found it and as he did so he glanced down into it. He stared in amazement. No wonder the old man had not wanted him to make tea in it! It was stuffed full of notes, not fivers, but ten and twenty pound notes.

"Blimey!" he gasped. Behind him the blankets stirred. "All right, I'm not going to take them," he said, putting the teapot back where he had found it.

He helped the sick man to drink the strong, sweet, milkless tea and it seemed to revive him, and perhaps in an effort to distract Tyso's mind from the money, he began to whisper to him, telling him how he came to be on his present site.

"This new farmer came along an' ordered me off where I'd bin fer years. Good place at the end of a drove*, sheltered by a ruined barn," he gasped. "Only shelter I could find was here. Wore me out, it did that move. Not a good place, this. Too near the dyke. Move on. In the spring. Yes. . . . In the spring."

The dog began to whine and the noise was so eerie that it made the hairs at the back of Tyso's neck prickle. He snarled at the dog to "shut up".

"Let 'un be. Its a good ol' dog. If it 'adn't bin fer the rabbits she caught, I'd 'ave starved to death this past week." The last word merged into a pitiful fit of coughing.

Tyso sat wondering what to do. Then he remembered the teapot full of money. There must be a town or village not too far away. He'd go and get some food; that should help. Perhaps he could get some cough medicine, only he wasn't

* track between a farm or farm buildings and main road.

quite so sure about that. He told his plan to the old man who, now too weak to protest, watched with agonised eyes as Tyso took a ten pound note from its hiding place and stuffed it into his pocket.

"Which way do I go?"

A trembling finger poked out from the bedclothes and pointed for a moment to the right before falling back limply onto the blankets.

"Won't be long," Tyso called as he set off, facing into the lashing rain.

It was a long, cold walk and he had only his instincts to guide him as he trudged along the top of the dyke exposed to all that the weather could hurl at him. Eventually, he came to a plank bridge. He crossed it, alarmed at the way that the water was only centimetres below the boards. Once on the other side, he found himself on a drove road at the far end of which he could see the faint shapes of huddled roofs. However, instead of feeling cheered at the sight, his heart felt heavier with every step that he took. He knew that he had money in his pocket and so he could pay his way, but he'd been turned out of shops enough times to dread the possible ordeal ahead.

He clenched his fist round the ten pound note and began to whistle softly to himself.

The street was strangely quiet, even for a wet day. For a moment Tyso considered the possibility that this God forsaken corner of England in which he had landed up might be rather short of people. But then he heard them, the church bells, pealing out for morning service as they had done every Sunday for countless years, regardless of sun, regardless of rain, regardless of gale, calling the faithful. The same sound was the signal for chapel goers to walk to the other end of the village for their service.

Tyso just couldn't believe it, Sunday. After walking all that way! He'd forgotten it must be Sunday. It was pouring with rain, indeed it was even worse than before, and he turned up his jacket collar in a vain attempt to stop the water dripping off his hair and down his neck, whilst with every step that he took the water in his shoes squelched.

Whereas a few minutes before he had dreaded going into a shop, he now longed for the chance to do so. He passed three shops, the blinds pulled down tautly, like the eyelids of dead men, Tyso thought. He shivered and turned back the way he had come.

Worshippers were hurrying by in both directions, buried deep in the protection of umbrellas and far too preoccupied with keeping dry to notice the gypsy boy. The squat, unattractive houses that stood shoulder to shoulder against the pavement showed no signs of life behind their lace curtains, other than one bedraggled canary in a cage. One house was double fronted with a brass plate outside. It might have been a doctor's house or surgery.

Tyso stared with unseeing eyes at the blank windows. He knew that the old man back in the bender tent needed good food and medicine. He'd half promised himself to find a way of getting cough medicine. He knew little about such things because Gran had usually doctored the whole family. She knew all that there was to know about herbs and things like that, although his mother had sometimes hidden these potions away and produced red or brown stuff from the shops. Not that they needed medicine often; they were a tough lot. Tyso felt a stabbing pang of sadness. The past was so far away, so lost.

He was quite unaware that he was standing in the middle of the road, and oblivious of the fact that a car had drawn up before the house with the brass plate. A man got out of the car and hurried to the door where he stood fumbling for his key. It was then that he caught sight of the bedraggled boy.

"I'd advise you to get out of the rain," he called cheerfully. It gave him a chance to look more closely at the lad whom he did not recognise. All, or almost all, the people round here were fair, but this one was decidedly dark – gypsy dark. Odd. He hadn't heard that there were gypsies in the district, and as a JP he would most certainly have heard if there had been. He

13

was only too accustomed to the accusations of chicken thefts and filthy litter that always resulted from a visit by the travelling people. This one was staring at him with the look, part-insolent, part-whipped, that is the hallmark of his race.

4

If Dr Davies had not worked in the fens for a number of years and so learnt to be very patient and observant, he might well have stepped into the warm, dry hallway of his house and left the boy gaping at his front door and shiny brass plate. As it was, he remained looking at the bedraggled stranger. The boy's lips were slightly apart as if he had started to speak and lost courage. On his face was all the uncertainty that is common on the faces of those in their early teens for whom life is proving rather too full of problems, but also there was that other, elusive look, that 'gypsy look'.

The guttering by the roof finally gave up the unequal battle with the rain and poured over in a cascade, only just missing Tyso, who leapt sideways in the nick of time. Although he had jumped to the side he was still staring, staring at the black leather case that the man was holding. He ran his tongue over his lips and drew in his breath, but no words came.

"What is it, lad? What do you want?" Clearly the boy did want something.

Tyso dragged a hand from his pocket. Very slowly he pointed at the bag. His jaw worked steadily but no sound came. His tongue could be quick, too quick at times, but that was when he was defending himself, or outsmarting some gaujo. This was different.

"Well, out with it lad. What do you want?"

There was an unhealthy moan to the wind and the leaden sky threatened even more storms. There had been more flood warnings and, despite the air of calm Dr Davies knew that behind the lace curtained windows treasured possessions were being carried upstairs and carpets were being rolled up in preparation for the flood that had been forecast. In a number of houses the elderly were making their painful way

15

up the stairs to rooms that had been left uninhabited since the last flood several years before. The able-bodied would be needed in the hours to come, either working on the dyke walls or rescuing people from the outlying farms, and Dr Davies wanted some food before it all began. He sighed, but he waited. Eventually the lad would speak.

Tyso looked to left and right to make quite sure that he had a line of retreat. He swallowed hard.

"You're a doctor. Right?" It was out. The question was asked.

"Yes. My name's Davies, Dr Davies. What's the matter? Can I help?"

The world hadn't changed. The rain was still pouring down. The sky was still grey and low and threatening, but Tyso felt a surge of relief, as though sunlight had burst through the rain and was swelling down the road.

"Well?" asked the doctor, trying hard to keep the irritation out of his voice.

"Yes".

Dr Davies took this to mean that he could be of use so he put the key in the lock, and looking back over his shoulder at Tyso said, "You had better come inside. At this rate we both stand a good chance of catching pneumonia.

"Now", he said, once they were out of the rain and in the hall, "what is this all about?"

Tyso took a deep breath and explained as best he could all about the bender tent and the old man who was so ill, and food and the medicine and it being Sunday. When he had finished speaking the doctor nodded. "I know who you mean. Ike Herne. He's quite a local character. I had no idea that he'd moved on. We'd better go to him at once. I'm afraid that if the dykes are breached he won't stand a chance. Have you dried out?" He paused. "Did you tell me your name?" Tyso shook his head. "Are you going to?"

He waited.

"Tyso Boswell," Tyso mumbled reluctantly. He didn't like giving his name to people. It wasn't their business. It had nothing to do with them. However, this man seemed to expect it and he must be kept sweet if he was going to be any use. No point in rubbing him up the wrong way; no point at all.

The journey back to the bender tent was in the doctor's car and followed a different route to the one that Tyso had taken earlier. When they got out of the car, they were near another bridge wider than the one Tyso had used but he recognised the spot. They stood on the bank and looked across at where the bender tent should have been and Tyso cried out in horror. Only grey swirling water, only lashing rain, only some floating debris; of the sick old man and his frail home nothing remained. The waters had found the weak point in the dyke and had torn through while Tyso stood indecisively in the village street.

"My God!" Dr Davies muttered. "Poor old Ike."

There was nothing that they could do. The bridge was well awash and quite impassable. They ran along the top of the dyke desperately hoping that Ike might somehow have been washed to their side, or perhaps near enough to be dragged from the water, but they both knew it was hopeless. The flood water would have swirled down upon him and washed him out across the fields. There was nothing that they could do. As they drew level with the place where the tent had once stood, the utter hopelessness of the situation was only too obvious.

"It's no good," Dr Davies said at last. "I must go back to the village. There's work to do." He turned and walked away and Tyso trudged along behind him.

The rain now drove onto their faces and ran down their cheeks like tears. They would be the only tears shed for Ike Herne and perhaps it was right that it should be the elements that should seem to mourn his passing. After all, it was among them, and not men, that he had lived out his life. Tyso had a dim sense of this, a vague awareness that in the end, perhaps, all things were for the best. Ike would have been miserable if they had put him into a hospital. As it was, he had died as he had lived, independent to the last of the bureaucratic world of the modern gaujo. Yes, all in all, Tyso decided, it was for the best. A good way to live: a good way to die. A dream that had

17

begun the night before embedded itself further into his mind.

"No more trailers for me," he thought. "No more lay-bys and waste-ground behind factories, and certainly no more gaujo houses."

By now they had reached the car and Dr Davies was holding the door open.

"No thanks, I'll be off."

"Hold on." Dr Davies sounded firm. "There is no way that I'm leaving you out here. Get in, at once."

Tyso was surprised and very annoyed to find that he was doing as he was told.

"Where do you come from? Can I take you anywhere?" Dr Davies asked. Tyso shook his head.

"You must belong somewhere."

Thinking quickly, Tyso replied, "I'm going to my aunty about ten miles on. I must get to her. She'll be worrying something awful."

"You stick around for a bit, and as soon as I've sorted out one or two matters, I'll see if we can't organise some transport. Lives Metford way, does she?" Tyso had no idea where Metford was but he reckoned that the doctor was shortly going to be far too busy to worry about him so he just nodded, and decided to wait his chance to slip away. No one was going to take him anywhere.

He was quite right. Dr Davies was extremely busy immediately he reached the village and as soon as his back was turned Tyso was off. Floods or no floods, he was getting away.

He walked for miles along roads lapped by flood water. Occasionally a lorry full of men with sand bags drove past him but otherwise there was hardly any traffic, and anyone who did pass him was occupied by their own problems and gave no thought to a gypsy youth trudging grimly forward.

As the day drew to a close, he was ravenously hungry and extremely tired and it seemed like a miracle when he came across a house that stood just above flood level. There were no lights and a cautious inspection proved that it was empty. A little clever manipulation of a window latch and Tyso was soon inside.

It was obvious that the house had been abandoned as the flood had drawn close for a fire still flickered in the open grate. It never occurred to Tyso that the owners had just gone out for a while. It wasn't that sort of day. The flood ruled people's behaviour and these people had fled the flood.

He found food in the larder and ate as he warmed himself by the fire. He didn't turn on the light as he had no wish to attract attention. There was a sofa in front of the fire, and so he helped himself to a couple of blankets from upstairs, and settled down on it to sleep.

5

Tyso blinked. Bright sunlight filled the room, but that was not what had awoken him. He found himself staring up into the face of a policeman whose hand was firmly gripping his shoulder.

"Had a good night, old son?" the policeman asked, curling his tongue round the question in such a way as to fill it with menace.

"Enjoyed yourself on the Brown's sofa, have you? Had a good meal too, by the look of things."

"I ain't done nothing," Tyso snarled, as he wriggled in the policeman's grip.

"Breaking and entering, laddie. That's what you did. Breaking and entering."

"That's daft." Tyso began, and then he remembered the window.

"That's enough of your lip, gyppo." The policeman cuffed Tyso on the ear and pulled him from the sofa. "On your feet, then."

Tyso struggled upright and, still struggling, was pulled to the patrol car waiting outside. Another policeman stood there waiting for them.

"I see you got him, Fred," he said. "Gyppo by the looks of him. Lucky we thought to check out this place, otherwise God knows what the Browns would have found when they got back." He cuffed Tyso for good measure, and bundled him into the back of the car. Fred got in beside him.

Tyso was accustomed to the inside of police stations. They were to him what airport lounges are to more sophisticated people, not in themselves alarming but nonetheless threaded through with the possibility of troubles and difficulties, impossible to anticipate or prevent. What did worry him was the thought of being in a detention centre. He could not bear the idea of being shut away, of losing his freedom. The policeman's tunic scratched against his face, cold and unyielding.

Prison.

Shut in.

The pit of Tyso's stomach heaved in sympathy with his thoughts. The countryside was a blur. He must act quickly. Once inside the nick there was no chance at all.

Ideas were rapidly forming inside his dark head, stirring at the roots of memory. The whining voices of women out to get rags or sell worthless trinkets to suspicious housewives, and the snivelling voices of men pleading for a pitch for their trailer, these were the survival tricks of his race. "'Er Mister," his voice mimicked the voices in his memory, "let us go, then. Honest, Mister, I won't give yer any more trouble. I'm movin' on see, movin' on," his voice rose, "that's what I'm doin'. Movin' out of the county like. Back to me folks. Me mum's ill and me dad . . ." His voice broke effectively and he gulped, "me dad's cleared out, see. Let us go, please Mister, please."

The policeman in the back of the car grinned at him whilst the shoulders of the driver heaved in mock amusement.

"I know and your sister is in trouble and your kid brother has gone and broken his leg."

Tyso swore softly in a language that the others could not know and their laughter turned sour and was still.

As their journey continued in silence, Tyso felt more desperate with every moment that passed. He could already hear the clang of the cell door and the echoing rattles of metal in confined spaces, and all the while his stomach was playing unpleasant tricks on him. It was this that gave him an idea. He watched out of the front window and when he saw some trees ahead he turned again to the policeman beside him and said, "I feel sick."

The policeman ignored him.

He tried again. "I feel sick."

Still the policeman ignored him.

"If you don't stop, I'll be sick all over your shoes," he said in a strangled voice, heaving forward to demonstrate his point.

"Blimey," the man swore, "why is it always me? Here Harry," he leant forward and tapped the driver on the shoulder, "matey says he's going to be sick. Stop the car. I can't face another 'do' this week."

Harry pulled the patrol car into the side and braked. Beside them the trees loomed helpfully.

Fred got out and Tyso, bent almost double now and with his hand across his mouth, followed him. He leant against the car.

"Not over the car, gyppo." Fred pushed him away slightly. Tyso's lowered head butted him hard in the stomach and sent him reeling and gasping, and Tyso was away, making for the trees as fast as he could go. Once there he slithered between them as silently and efficiently as a fox. Bushes hardly stirred where he had passed and if a twig snapped it was quite lost in the thundering noise of his blaspheming pursuers. After a few minutes he doubled back on his tracks and dropped down on the grass by the road. Cautiously he lifted his head. There was only the abandoned patrol car; nothing else was in sight. With weasel-like agility he darted across the road and scrambled down the bank towards the water beyond it. There he stopped, driving in his toes and clinging to the brown grass.

After what seemed an age, he heard the two men return. Their boots rang on the tarmac, and this sound was followed by the murmur of Harry's voice as he talked to the station, presumably reporting the escape. My God! Would they send out dogs to look for him? He wouldn't be able to shake off dogs. Now Harry was talking to Fred. Tyso strained to hear what they were saying.

"There's a scare on. Some bloke's broken from custody at the Magistrates' Court. We're recalled."

"Yes, but what about matey?"

"What about him? No time to bother with him now. We'll deal with him later."

22

Fred snorted.

"Come on," Harry said, "this other one's a right tearaway by the sound of it."

"I wouldn't call matey here sweetness and light, and besides, I'd like to get my hands on him, if only for a couple of minutes."

"You'll get the chance. He'll turn up some time. His sort always do."

Car doors banged. The engine revved. They were gone and Tyso was violently sick.

6

Having scrambled up the bank, Tyso went back to the woods and hurried through them to the other side. There was no flooding here and he was able to cut across the country for several miles, thus avoiding roads where he feared that he might be picked up from a description. If he came upon an isolated cottage or farm, he skirted round it, and so he passed the day without meeting anyone, and by late afternoon he had put many miles between himself and the place where he had escaped from the police. However, he had had nothing to eat since the night before and he was very hungry. It would soon be dark too, and once again he had nowhere to sleep.

Tyso sat on a gate and stared gloomily around him. He had no idea where he was going. It was cold. The puddles in the carts' ruts were glazing over with a thin sheet of ice. It was no night for sleeping in the open. Once, years ago when he was young, he had been walking along by a spinney one bright frosty morning when he had noticed a pair of boots sticking out from under a hedge. Naturally curious, he had investigated further and found the body of a tramp, hoar frost still in his hair and his eyes fringed with droplets like tears. Tyso had rushed home to tell Dad about it, but his father had said that such things were best left alone; it didn't do to get mixed up in things like that.

The next year they were again in that area and Tyso found himself walking by the same spinney. He'd looked for the boots but they had gone. However, on looking closer, he'd seen among the green mosses and brown leaves the glint of white bones. Whoever had taken the boots had obviously agreed with Dad.

Tyso wished that he hadn't remembered that just now. Of course, it wasn't going to be all that cold! It was better than a cell, anyway. He ran a hand through his dark hair and laughed in the dusk at the thought of how he'd tricked the policeman. Anyone out on those lonely fen fields that evening could have been forgiven for believing that it was some evil spirit sitting there laughing in the engulfing silence.

"Can't stay here," he muttered to himself eventually as his fingers began to grow numb with the cold. He jumped down from the gate and strode on manfully, whistling to keep up his courage. He needed that courage for there was no sign of a place for him to shelter and it was now almost dark.

Far ahead lights flickered, two or three at first and then a number of them. Tyso hurried on towards them, often stumbling on the rough ground as he went. Somehow, it no longer seemed quite so important to avoid roads and houses. What did matter was not being stranded in this unfriendly countryside where not even a hedge offered shelter.

At last he was at the edge of the village. He scrambled onto the road and walked silently along the single, poorly lit street. On either side the glow of curtained windows shut him out. The white light of television screens and the muffled music from transistors and music centres also mocked his loneliness. The outsider was where he belonged, outside. Stealthily, alert to any danger, he walked on.

A cat, streaking from one side of the road to the other, was caught momentarily in a patch of light and then melted into the darkness again.

Halfway along the street was a pub. The warm smell of beer hung in the air around its drab walls and peeling sign. It appeared to be a place without life, one of those pubs that only come to life on a Saturday night. However, something there did catch Tyso's eye. Leaning up against the wall was a bike, not a smart racing job, all chrome and paint and optional extras, but just a plain, rather battered, man's bike. If it had been expensive, Tyso would have left it strictly alone, it would have been too risky to do otherwise. He walked over to it and checked that it was not locked. Then, having glanced to left and right to make sure that there was no one about, he cycled speedily away. At the end of the village street he stopped and put on the lights, and pedalled off into the night.

In a couple of miles a barn loomed out of the darkness. Tyso stopped to explore it. The door was ajar and, by the light of the bicycle lamp, he could see that it was well supplied with hay. It was with a sigh of relief that he went inside and pulled the door shut after him. It was only a matter of minutes before he had made himself comfortable and had fallen asleep.

If there was anything that he should have noticed, he failed to see it. He was worn out, and dead to the night.

Tyso was itching all over from his hay bed. He stretched and scratched, scratched and stretched, easing himself gently back into the sun-bathed world, for sunlight was pouring into the barn from the open doorway. He sat up. He'd shut the door. He distinctly remembered shutting the door. If he'd shut it, who had opened it? He scrambled to his feet, half expecting a policeman to seize him. Nothing happened. Sparrows twittered happily in the rafters overhead. Tyso stared round him, peering anxiously into the murky, cobwebbed corners.

A shadow fell across the light from the doorway. Tyso clenched his fists. This time he'd make a proper fight of it. The diminutive figure of a small girl of about four or five stood there, dark curls straying from under the hood of her anorak.

"Daddy says you might as well both come in for your breakfasts rather than light a fire and send us all up in flames, and hurry 'cos it's ready." And with this the tiny but extremely articulate messenger went as suddenly as she had come.

Tyso stared at the door in amazement and tried to sort out the confusion in his mind. He must have missed the house in the dark. That made sense, especially if it was beyond the barn. But 'both of you'. Both of who? The kid could have got it wrong, but it was a strange thing to say. Then, it was all strange. Invited to breakfast! "Both come in for your breakfasts", that was what she had said.

"Hi!" The voice came from nearby and Tyso almost screamed with shock. He looked around again, but saw no one.

"Looks like breakfast comes with bed here, don't it?"

Tyso gasped for the voice was definitely coming from above him. He looked up. No wonder the sparrows had been chirping so busily. They must have been very surprised to have such company, for there, perched securely in a fork of the supporting beam, sat a lad a year or so older than Tyso. He had straight, light brown hair, a rather thin face with sharp features which was well peppered with spots. His longish nose and narrow blue eyes gave him something of a fox-like appearance. His jeans were very shabby and patched, and his faded red and grey tartan jacket, with its dirty fleecy lining, was also very worn. However, he had a smile that made up for a great deal, the kind of smile that one feels is worth waiting to see.

"Stand clear. I'm baling out."

Tyso leapt aside as the other fell heavily into the hay beside him. He stood up at once.

"Blimey, the country isn't half a dirty place to live," he said, brushing cobwebs and hay from his clothes and hair. "Saw you arrive last night," he went on cheerfully. "What's your name?"

Tyso didn't answer. Tell someone your name and there was no telling where it might end.

"Mine's Andy."

"Tyso," Tyso found himself saying, "mine's Tyso."

"Tyso. What sort of name is that?" Andy laughed.

Tyso shrugged. The situation was altogether too much for him.

"You must be a gyppo."

Tyso felt his anger surging up, but at least this was something he understood: something that he could handle.

27

"Want to make something of it?" he shouted.

"No," Andy said, rather disappointingly. "I want my breakfast. Come on."

"You're not going, are you?" Tyso was appalled at the idea.

"'Course I am. I'm hungry . . ."

"But, but . . ."

"You don't have to come, but I'm going," and Andy went to the door.

"Here, wait for me." Tyso hurried after him. He was hungry too.

7

The farmhouse was the usual grey square fen building surrounded by its cluster of outbuildings of which the barn was one.

They went across the yard, their shoes scrunching on the frost hard mud, and found the back door which stood slightly open.

"Buck up. We can't wait all day," a man's voice called as they stood hesitating outside.

They went in.

A tall, well-built man sat at the head of the table. He was in early middle age and his fair hair was greying at the temples. The small girl was also there as was a girl in her middle teens.

"Ah, so you've come at last. Well sit yourselves down and get stuck in." The man nodded towards two empty chairs and they sat down. They ate ravenously and in silence. Tyso had had no idea of how hungry he was until then.

After they had eaten, the man, who had been watching them keenly throughout the meal, said, "I'm not one to ask questions and if you two want to move on, fair enough and I'll ask no more than a couple of hours work for your food, but if you want to rest a while I can find work for both of you. My only farm hand is past it, if the truth were told, and only turns up nowadays when he's short of beer money. Not but what he's a good old chap in his own way. So there you are. You can have board and lodgings and a wage, but by heck you'll have to work for it."

Tyso glanced at Andy who had kept his eyes down all the while, but now he looked sideways at the man and then at Tyso. "All right. Might as well stay a bit," he said, and Tyso nodded in agreement. After all, somewhere was better than nowhere, for the time being, anyway.

The back door opened slowly revealing an elderly, weather-scarred face erupting with stiff grey bristles and shaded by an incredibly battered felt hat. "Mornin' Mr Mellows, Miss Aileen, young Sue, sorry I'm late, but some 'un made off wi' me bike las' night." The man wobbled unsteadily across to the table. Tyso could hardly credit his bad luck.

"Oh Jack, it's always something," sighed Mr Mellows.

"Ah, but that's the truth, so help me," the old man said before gulping down the tea handed to him by the girl he'd called Miss Aileen. She was a pleasant looking girl, not exactly pretty, but attractive just the same, with long fair hair and soft, grey eyes.

"Let it be this time Jack." Mr Mellow nodded towards Tyso and Andy. "Names of?" and they both found themselves telling him. "Two new hands, best set them on mucking out the byre. You lads will find boots behind that door. There are several sizes to choose from," he added as he strode out into the yard.

For about an hour they struggled to shift the close-packed straw and manure, using their pitchforks with clumsy inexperience. Both were tired and irritable. The smell alone was enough to make them want to give up, but at least it was warm, Tyso thought.

"I'm knocking off for a fag," Andy said, sticking his pitchfork into the ground and diving a hand into an inside pocket of his jacket. "Have one?" He offered the packet to Tyso, expertly thrusting forward a cigarette with a flick of his wrist. Tyso shook his head, and went on half-heartedly poking at the evil smelling bedding.

"What the hell's the matter with you?" Andy asked. "You've not said a word all the time we've been out here, not a bleedin' word."

"Got something on my mind, haven't I."

"Who hasn't," Andy snorted climbing on to the byre fence and puffing contentedly. "It's that bike, isn't it?" he asked at last, his patience quite exhausted.

"What bike?" Tyso asked stupidly.

"Come off it! The bike that you brought into the barn last night."

Tyso glanced round anxiously to make sure that they had not been overheard.

"Well, isn't it?"

"Mebbe, mebbe not."

"You'd better move it from the barn before that Jack character finds it," Andy said, serious now. "Could lead to questions and things like that. I don't know for sure about you, but I'm not too keen on questions just now. I'm well, I'm lying a bit low at the moment."

Tyso nodded. "So am I. I'll have to get rid of that bike somehow."

"Tell you what . . ." Andy began but his voice faded away as he realised that Mr Mellows was standing only a few yards off.

"You, the dark one, Tyso is it? Come here a minute," he said.

Tyso's spirits sank down to the muck on his boots. He glanced round the byre instinctively searching for an escape route, but as he did so he walked towards the burly farmer.

"I want a letter posted and that means going into the village. There's an old bike turned up in the barn. I've a feeling it belongs down in the village. Best if you run it back there, probably save a lot of fuss and bother." He handed Tyso a brown envelope.

Feeling numb and confused, Tyso took the letter, went to the barn, got the bike and cycled to the village. Cars went by. People ignored him. It was as if no one was looking for Tyso Boswell. The wanted man wasn't wanted any more. Then it occurred to him that he was many miles away from where he had been arrested.

It was a lovely day, and now that the frost had gone you could feel the spring stirring in everything; not quite ready yet, waiting still, but growing restless. Tyso would have loved to have enjoyed it, to have taken pleasure in the sight of the first grey pussy willow buds and the clumps of snowdrops in the little grey churchyard, but he could not. Wasn't he, after

31

all, despite local indifference, still a hunted man, riding a stolen bicycle back to the place that he had taken it from? Then there was Mr Mellows and the farm. What was he doing there? Why had he agreed to stay?

The pub was ahead of him now. He propped the bike against the wall and turned back the way that he had come.

He began to whistle. Several birds were singing. He did wish that there were hedgerows in this part of England, that everything wasn't quite so flat and bleak. It had its own sort of beauty, though.

The drains*, which seemed to be everywhere, were full, and the one that flowed beside the road reflected the sky with its scurrying clouds. A heron, the old man of the fens, flopped across the sky ahead of him, its long legs trailing, streamer-like behind it. A kestrel hovered, stooped and rose clutching a small mouse in its talons. It was all very peaceful and a million miles away from the trailers and the scrap by the motorway.

Something moved in the grass by the roadside. Tyso stopped. He squatted down, staring intently at the grass.

He leapt forward, clamping down his hands over the gently vibrating grass blades. "Got yer!" he cried triumphantly and drew his cupped hands towards his chest. Very cautiously, he eased his hands open a crack and peered in.

The frog sat there, her green and brown sides swollen with unlaid spawn and her yellow underbelly glowing like sunlight in the dim cavern of his hands.

"Aren't you a beauty!" he murmured contentedly as he jumped up. Having removed his dikla† he wrapped it around the captive whom he then placed in a pocket. After that, well pleased with himself, he hurried back to the farm.

"Posted the letter all right?" Mr Mellows asked at dinner as he ladled out the rich brown stew, thick with carrots and onions and dotted with fluffy white dumplings.

Tyso stared at him. The letter! The brown envelope! He'd never posted it.

*a drainage ditch without banks   † small neck scarf

The walls of the room crowded in on him. The ceiling was too low. Were all gaujos' houses so stifling?

In his pocket, beneath the red dikla, the envelope nestled threateningly.

All those at the table seemed to be staring at him, awaiting his reply. He looked away, checking the distance to the back door, assuring himself of a line of retreat.

He gulped, trying to ease the sudden dryness in his mouth. "The letter?" he managed to say at last.

"Yes, lad, the letter." Mr Mellows didn't bother to conceal the irritation in his voice. "Posted it, have you?"

Tyso nodded. "Yup. It's gone." His voice didn't sound right to him – far too high and squeaky – but no one appeared to notice.

"Good, good," Mr Mellows said, and went back to dishing up the stew. For a moment he had wondered whether he hadn't been too impulsive in taking on the two young tearaways now consuming vast quantities of food at a remarkable rate. But it hadn't seemed to him that he had much choice. He wouldn't, couldn't turn away the young gyppo, and how could he keep one and kick out the other? He knew the face of trouble when he saw it. He'd give them both a chance for a few days, see what happened. He was glad about the letter and pleased with himself about the way in which he'd arranged the return of the bicycle. "No point in looking for problems," he thought.

After she had eaten, Susan slipped off her chair and came to stand a few feet away from Tyso. She gazed at him thoughtfully, but rather shyly, all her former boldness gone.

Tyso liked children. Gypsies have strong family ties and the confined space in which they live means that children are always on hand, scrambling about, getting under the grown-ups' feet like so many lurcher puppies, but almost always with someone to care for them, be it mother or grandmother, sister or brother. Tyso was missing Rosie and Edward. He missed them more deeply than even he knew. Their absence broke the pattern of his life far more severely than his adventures among the gaujos. He needed the warmth of their

33

bodies close to him as they sat before the yog. He needed the comfort of Edward curled on his lap as they watched television in the trailer, and the fun of Rosie dressing up in brilliant pieces of rag from the collection bags and strutting about 'like the Queen'. Of course, if someone had suggested that even after such a short time away he was already homesick, Tyso would have punched them senseless in an instant. Anyway, he would see them again, rescue them from Uncle Jo and Aunt Sarah. He'd promised that to himself.

Now Susan stood motionless, intrigued by the stranger with the large, sad brown eyes, dark hair and swarthy complexion.

Tyso wanted to speak but didn't know what to say.

Then he remembered the frog.

Very carefully, he eased it out of his dikla.

The child moved forward, fascinated by the jerking movements of the red cloth.

The brown envelope fluttered down at her feet like an injured sparrow.

At once there was a thud and Andy was on his knees beside her, an arm round her waist and looking at the dikla.

"What is it?" he asked in a dramatic voice. "Is it dangerous?"

The child shivered excitedly; and, somehow between the opening of the mysterious parcel and the bemused frog jumping out the brown envelope vanished.

8

The friendship between Andy and Tyso was firmly rooted in the incident of the brown envelope, which, incidentally, was posted a couple of days later. However, this friendship did not extend to asking each other how they came to be in the barn that night. They protected their pasts very carefully for it was the only way that they knew to protect their futures. Neither did they share the same accommodation. Tyso could not face the idea of sleeping in a house when the alternative of the barn was so readily available. So he carried his bedding out there and made himself comfortable among the hay, undisturbed by the nocturnal venturings of the mice and the early morning excitement of the sparrows. There, away from the home of the gaujos, he was able to dream of having his own vardo and being his own man.

During the day he worked beside Andy on the farm, with little time to consider the man they worked for, or his motherless family. They learned through conversations that Mr Mellows had not always been a farmer. The farm had belonged to his father, and it was only on his death that Mr Mellows had returned to run it. Secretly, Tyso held him in some contempt. Still, it suited him to stick around for a while, and the food was good.

Friday night was pay night, and if the money in their pockets wasn't generous, it was fair.

"I'll be going down to the village this evening," Mr Mellows announced after they had eaten. "Darts match," he added.

"Dad's captain of the team," Aileen explained. Now that she had left school her life was very much wrapped up in the life of the farm and the house.

"Yes, well, if you two would like a lift to the village," Mr

35

Mellows continued, somewhat embarrassed by this reference to his captaincy, "I'll be going at about seven. There's something on in the Village Hall, I think. Disco. Saw a notice about it last week. Chance to look over some of the local talent, anyway," and he winked.

Tyso and Andy looked at each other. "Might as well," they agreed.

"You going?" Andy asked Aileen casually as they waited for Mr Mellows to collect his darts from the front room.

"No. I have to stay with Susan."

Andy jerked his head in acknowledgement of this fact, dug his hands deep into the pockets in the front of his jacket and glowered at his toe caps.

"Come along, you two. I can't wait all evening," roared the captain of the darts team, eager for the fray.

He left them outside the Village Hall.

"Pick you up at eleven, unless you'd rather walk back," he said as they stood shivering in the roadway.

"We'll be here," Andy said firmly. He didn't fancy the idea of the long dark walk home, facing a cold head wind. Tyso didn't say anything. He was already regretting that he had come.

Music blared out, and huddles of dark figures could be seen leaning against the wooden walls of the hut, their faces occasionally illuminated for a few seconds by the uncertain light of a flickering match. Motor bikes were parked in clusters and gleamed menacingly when caught in the head-lights of new arrivals. A group of girls were standing under the porch light, quite aware that they were the focus of attention, despite the fact that none of the boys seemed to have so much as noticed that they were there.

Whenever Tyso had been to a disco, he'd been with a crowd of friends, boys whose families he travelled with. In a body, they would saunter in, conscious of the sensation caused by their arrival, the effect of their dark good looks on the girls, and the bristling antagonism of the boys. Occasionally they danced, but more often they just watched and, almost invariably, they ended up fighting with the gaujos on

36

one pretext or another. It was usually something to do with a girl, and always it was something to do with the fact that they were 'gyppos'. That was fine. That was Saturday evening out. Here he was alone, well except for Andy, and he'd never seen him fight.

However, his friend was already moving towards the entrance, hands thrust, casually now, into his jacket pockets. Tyso followed him and in doing so set off a string of events the consequences of which he could not even begin to imagine.

9

The girls in the doorway made a poor pretence of not noticing them; strangers were rare indeed.

They paid their money to a man sitting at a card table and became part of the pulsing lights and music. They walked slowly round the room, watching the handful of dancers and reached the trestles that formed the bar at the back of the hall.

"Beer," Andy said.

"No alcohol," replied the barman without looking up from the glass that he was wiping on the corner of a rather grubby butcher's blue striped apron that he was wearing.

"Blimey," snarled Andy, "what's this then? Bleedin' Sunday School outing?"

"No alcohol," the barman repeated without any change in the tone of his voice, and still without bothering to look up.

"Marvellous!" Andy said, conveying, he hoped, the impression that these clodhopping locals were completely out of touch with the throbbing modern world. However, his tone did not appear to have the desired effect for, looking up briefly before returning to his glass polishing, the barman only said, "You're under age, anyway. Have a coke or go without."

"Under age. That's what you say!" Andy retorted defiantly, but he bought a coke, and Tyso did too.

They watched for a while, pretending not to notice the curious glances, and trying not to feel too isolated from those around them, most of whom had known each other from childhood. Andy was apparently content to go on watching but Tyso was not. He was a good dancer and he knew it. He decided that it was time someone showed these country bumpkins how it was done!

Most of the girls were congregated at the other end of the

room, whispering together and laughing over their shoulders to obtain the maximum effect. Tyso mentally selected a blonde with a tiny waist and a tight fitting tee-shirt. He rearranged himself slightly against the trestle bar and waited patiently for her to be aware of him. It didn't take long. Soon he was dancing happily, oblivious of everything except the tiny waist and the tight tee-shirt.

A well-built muscular young man wearing a great deal of black leather studded with metal in various shapes and forms ambled on to the floor. He tapped Tyso on the shoulder, and then, jerking a thumb over his shoulder said, "On your way. Viv here goes with me."

"Oh Dave," Viv simpered.

Tyso stopped dancing and glared, his dark eyes flashing with the instinctive fire of battle. "Get lost," he hissed back through clenched teeth, "or do you want to make something of it?"

"Outside." A couple of large men had loomed on to the scene, and Tyso, who was something of an expert in such matters, realised that he was about to be bounced.

"All right. All right. I'm going, aren't I!" There was no point in pushing his luck. It was best to lie low for a time, even though he longed to smash his fist into the grinning face of the older boy. He went to the door and Andy, also anxious to avoid trouble, followed him.

Scarcely had they reached the centre of the car park, when a voice called to them from the doorway of the hall, "Here, gyppo, mind how you go, but keep going." A roar of laughter swelled out above the din of the music.

Tyso stopped and looked back at the young men arrogantly lounging in the lit porch, secure in their numbers. He saw Viv clinging to Dave's arm. She was laughing too. He ambled back across the car park. Slowly he approached the group. He stood in front of Dave, insolently measuring him with his eyes. After a moment he curled back his lips in a slow, almost dreamy, sneer, "Don't worry about me, flower," he said, his voice softly caressing the words. And Tyso raised his fists.

The minutes that followed were remarkable for several

reasons but not least for the total break down of pack law.

No one went to Dave's aid. They just stood there while blow after blow found its painful mark on his well-protected body. When Tyso, satisfied at last, delivered the *coup de grâce*, a punishing jab to the jaw, Dave toppled to the dust with no more than a low moan of surprise.

It was summed-up rather well by one of the by-standers who gasped, "Gawd, how the hell did that happen?"

Tyso stepped back and, head slightly on one side, surveyed his victim. With slow deliberation he ground the knuckles of one hand into the palm of the other, and then turned and walked away.

No one moved. They watched him walk off to join Andy and vanish into the darkness.

Tyso felt good. He'd won. Here, at this moment in time, he was the big guy. He, Tyso Boswell, gypsy of no fixed address, had won his fight. The clean fen air smelt sweet and cooled him pleasantly. He couldn't help swaggering slightly and whistling.

"Me dad used to fight a bit," he volunteered after a moment or two, feeling that his companion was not being quite appreciative enough. Receiving no response, he glanced sideways and found to his astonishment that Andy was not there.

"Where are you?" he called, suddenly feeling very vulnerable. No answer. He stood quite still in the middle of the street, staring around him. "Where've you gone?" Nothing stirred; not even a cat slunk by.

The Village Hall was still pumping out sound, but the darkness prevented him from seeing what was happening there. Ahead he saw the pub, light streaming from the windows. A car was parked on the edge of this slash of light, but by looking more carefully Tyso was able to see that it was a police patrol car. Now he knew why Andy was nowhere in sight. Also, he now understood . . . But himself, what about himself? His legs didn't seem to belong to him. He remembered the feel of the policeman's uniform.

He remembered knocking him over. What did you get for assaulting a policeman?

The door of the pub opened and Mr Mellows appeared in the company of two police officers.

"No," Tyso heard him say, "not here. Up at the Hall, more than likely. That's where your fight will be."

The men got into the car and the full headlights were switched on. Tyso was dazzled by the sudden glare.

"That you, Tyso?" called Mr Mellows. "A fight's been reported. Know anything about it?"

Tyso shook his head.

"Never one of yours, Bill?" enquired one of the policemen.

"No," replied Mr Mellows. "Both girls, as a matter of fact. This is a new hand I've taken on."

"Well we'd best get up to the Hall, though, with any luck they'll have sorted themselves out by now. See you sometime Bill."

The patrol car moved off and somewhere among the shadows Andy breathed a sigh of relief.

"What are you doing Tyso?" Mr Mellows called as he turned back into the pub.

Tyso shrugged. "Some fresh air. That's all."

Mr Mellows went back to his team.

"They've all gone," Tyso called softly into the night.

"Might come back. I'll stay for a while," Andy replied.

"Where are you? I'm coming with you."

It was not long before the white patrol car slid menacingly past them and out into the empty fen countryside. Shortly after that Mr Mellows emerged victorious from the pub and they joined him for the drive home.

He drove quickly and they were soon turning into the farm.

They were all too tired to notice the black Rolls Royce that had followed them from the village and now slowed down at the farm entrance before shooting off into the seemingly endless fen darkness.

41

10

The next day, being Sunday, they did not have to help on the farm. Tyso decided to go for a walk. Andy, a town boy through and through, tolerated the countryside as an unfortunate necessity. He saw no reason for actually enjoying it; he preferred to stay at home.

It was a beautiful early March day. The sky was clear, the air crisp and you could see for miles. Tyso had meant to walk through this new year world, but, as it happened, he didn't get very far. As he was leaving the farm buildings, his quick eyes noticed a series of movements in the grass and he set off in pursuit of another frog. His chase took him behind an outlying shed, a very decrepit affair.

He stopped. Amazed. He blinked. He couldn't believe it. Try as he might, he couldn't believe it. There, crumbling away from years of neglect, but, for all that, easily identifiable, stood a gypsy vardo.

"Blimey!" he managed to gasp at last.

Very slowly, almost timidly, he went towards it. Step by step he crossed over the rough ground, putting down his feet with cat-like movements, as if he feared that a booby trap might go off if he wasn't careful.

The vardo was in a dreadful state of disrepair. Its shafts were damaged, its sides breached in several places, the shutters and door hung off their hinges and all the elaborate decoration was rotten and crumbling. Tyso didn't see any of this. He saw a vardo; his dream, his tomorrow.

He sat down on a broken shaft and gazed and gazed. In all his life he'd seen no more than half-a-dozen vardos, and one of these he had watched burn as, its owner dead, the relatives followed the old ways and destroyed it along with his other possessions. How it had flamed in the dark night! How the

42

scatters of red sparks had glow-wormed, falling among damp leaves, glimmering and dying. He had never forgotten. People had come for hundreds of miles for the funeral and the fire that followed it, and they had stood silently around the crackling blaze. It was one of his relatives, a Boswell, they had buried that day, and Tyso had felt proud.

And now here was a vardo. It was up to him to get it for himself.

Getting it for himself seemed a small problem at first. In the first flush of excitement it all seemed perfectly possible, in fact, easy. But as he sat there thinking about it, seeing the vardo come together like one of those demolition films run backwards, he began to realise that it was by no means as easy as he had originally believed. As the problems crowded in he noticed that he was feeling cold.

He stood up and went to peer inside. It was filthy, a mass of dead leaves, pieces of sacking, straw wisps and spiders' webs. It was beautiful.

"I'll think of a way," he murmured to himself. "Somehow, I'll have it for myself."

He went in and poked around for a few minutes, trying to open the jammed cupboards and imagining what it had been like when it was furnished. He could see the bright brasses, the highly coloured materials and the plastic flowers in their cut glass vase . . . He could hear the shouts of the children as they laughed and squabbled in the confined space. When he thought of the children, his mind raced back to Rosie and Edward. "They won't half love this," he thought out loud, and, as he said it, he knew, knew with every fibre of his being, that one day they would be there beside him.

Eventually, he jumped down from the vardo and reluctantly walked away from it. He wasn't thinking where he was going; he was too busy planning how to take over the wreck behind him.

"Morning, chavvo*."

Tyso stopped.

Parked in the farmyard, out of sight of the house, was a large, black Rolls Royce, and leaning beside it was a sinewy

---

* boy /child,   chavvies = boys /children

looking man with a swarthy complexion and lank black hair. He was wearing a sheepskin coat and a long, expensive looking, blue silk scarf. His shoes gleamed in the sunlight. He was in the process of lighting a cigarette with a very expensive lighter. All in all, he was not the sort of person that one would expect to see on a remote fen farm on a quiet Sunday morning, nor at any other time for that matter.

For Tyso, however, the shock was not his appearance, flashy and well-off as it obviously was, he'd seen such people all his life. No for him the shock lay in meeting a gypsy and, what is more, one who greeted him as a gypsy.

The first thought that passed through his mind was that, somehow, his uncle had found out where he was and had sent the man to catch him and take him back to the North. The thought was so horrible that Tyso wasted no time in trying to reason it out, but swinging round, started to race off in the direction from which he had come, only to find his way barred by two other men who must have been standing almost parallel with him. These men grabbed him firmly by the arms and, try as he might, he could not shake them off.

"Leave me alone, will yer," he snarled as he tried to kick his captors on the shins.

"Stand still or I'll send you from here into the middle of next week," answered one of them, giving Tyso's arms an extra wrench, just for good measure.

"Bring him over here," ordered the man by the car.

Tyso was hauled, still struggling, towards the Rolls Royce.

"So you're the one who could punch his way out of anything, are you?" asked the man grinning.

Tyso swore in a stream of Romany that left his tormentor laughing so much that the ash on his cigarette spilled all over his sheepskin coat.

"The trouble with you youngsters is that you waste your energy," he laughed. "Let him go. Then clear off and keep an eye out for anyone coming along. Mr Hellfire here and I have some business to discuss . . . some fighting business."

Fighting business! So this man was nothing to do with uncle! But fighting business, what did he mean by that?

The two men released Tyso who shook himself like an angry terrier who had been held too long on the leash.

The men eased their shoulders and ambled off.

"Get into the car. I want to talk to you."

His curiosity thoroughly aroused, Tyso went round and got into the passenger seat.

"That's better," said the man, sliding in behind the driving wheel. "Like her, do you? Had it customised, you know; the odd detail here and there." The man smiled contentedly. He was out to impress and considered that he was doing rather well.

"Not bad. Seen better," Tyso replied, not quite truthfully.

"Got one of your own?" asked the man without a flicker of expression to show that he was joking.

"No, not likely."

"Fancy one?"

Tyso gave a characteristic shrug of his shoulders.

"Only I might be able to put you in the way of earning the right kind of money, eventually. But I'd better introduce myself. Name's Lee. Nathan Lee. Nat to my friends. Mr Lee to you. Yours?"

Tyso shrugged again.

For a full half minute the car was grave quiet. Tyso could not bring himself to say his name 'just in case', and the man seemed content to wait indefinitely for the answer. Then, very slowly, he drew out a wallet. It was full of twenty pound notes. It was beautiful. He fingered through the notes for a moment and then put away the wallet.

"Tyso. My name's Tyso Boswell," Tyso said in a thin voice that did not seem to belong to him.

Nathan Lee smiled, his teeth gleaming white in the tanned face, "Well, Tyso Boswell," he said softly, "I'm about to turn you into a rich chavvo with no problems."

11

A beautifully decorated vardo, pulled by a black grai*, went silently between the may-laden hedges accompanied by the song of sky-larks. There was money in the teapot in the cupboard, and Rosie sat with Edward on her lap. Tyso smiled contentedly, and the man beside him who dealt so much in deceit and greed, waited patiently for the idea of money to sink into his companion's mind.

At last he said, "I was passing through the village last night. Happened to see you. That was something! I've seen a lot of fighting in my time but seldom seen anything as good as that punch of yours. Fought much, have you? Can't say I've ever heard of you."

The vardo drifted away into the distance, and Tyso hurtled back into the present.

"Only fight if I have to," he said, trying to get to grips with reality. What was all this about fighting, anyway?

"Never had any proper bouts, then?"

"No."

"Seen any bare fist fighting, have you?"

Again Tyso shook his head. "No, except when two people get mad at each other. I've seen a lot of that sort of fighting."

Nathan nodded. "Well, I'm looking for a likely chavvo to put up against one from further up country that I've heard about. He's to come over this way next week. I've found somewhere for the fight . . . good place . . . very quiet . . . not too far from here. We're not likely to be interrupted by the police out there. Travellers will be coming from all over the country. Then what happens? My fighter goes and breaks some ribs in a practice bout. If you'd like to make some easy money by taking his place all you have to do is say so. I'll give you . . ." Nathan Lee paused, weighing up the youth of his companion. "I'll give you twenty-five pounds to fight and a hundred if you win. I can't say fairer than that, can I?"

With that money he could do marvellous things to the vardo, and have plenty over. A hundred pounds was worth fighting for, for Tyso never even considered the possibility of losing.

"I'll do it," he said firmly.

"Good. Fight's Saturday. Three o'clock. Some of my people will pick you up at two. Remember bare-fist fighting is illegal. We don't want any unwelcome visitors. People bet heavily and they don't want to be interrupted, and if they are they are inclined to become very nasty towards those they think may have informed against them, and that would be you, I'd see that's what they thought, anyway. So be careful. Don't say a word. Got it?"

Tyso felt an uncomfortable knot forming in the pit of his stomach. He didn't like being threatened.

"Lie low and keep your mouth shut. No one knows about you so no one can get at you. Out of the car, now. I'm off."

Tyso got out of the car. The two henchmen appeared and joined Nathan Lee. The Rolls Royce purred out of the yard and away down the road.

Tyso took himself off to bed in the barn much earlier than usual. He wanted to be alone to think. He lay in his blankets on the hay and listened to the scratchings of the mice and the low, night-time moan of the wind as it roamed in and out of the cracks and crevices. Everything was racing round in his head; the whole confused situation that had suddenly become his life.

It wasn't that he didn't want to fight, and he most certainly wanted the money. It was just that there were risks. There was the risk that someone might recognise him and tell his uncle. Indeed, there was even a chance that his uncle might come to the fight himself. Then there was the risk that he might well run into trouble with the police. But there again, there was the money. What a difference that would make. All those lovely notes!

He was just falling asleep, his mind cluttered with thoughts of the vardo, when he heard voices talking softly outside the barn and two shadows crossed the moonlit gap at the bottom of the door. Andy and Aileen were walking in the yard. Sighing, though he wasn't quite sure why, he pulled the blankets up well over his head and went to sleep.

12

It took Tyso three days to pluck up the courage to ask Mr Mellows about the vardo. He tried to find out about it from Aileen but all that he learned from her was that it had been there for ages, "simply ages", and she had "no idea where it had come from".

At last, on the Wednesday, when he was helping Mr Mellows to mend a fence, Tyso drew a deep breath and, fixing his eyes on the remote blue horizon, said, "What's that old caravan thing doing back of the shed?"

It was meant to sound casual and uninformed. Old caravan indeed! However, it came out rather differently from what he had intended, and anyone could have told that he was anything but indifferent to the subject.

"Oh, you mean the old vardo," Mr Mellows said, straightening his back. "Thought you might notice it some time. There's a story about it. Want to hear it?" Tyso nodded, still trying to seem casual, although in fact his heart was pounding.

"Well some years ago now there was this fellow, see. Good-looking lad with a steady job. One day this lad's job took him to a gypsy encampment. It was an atchin' tan* that was used a good deal."

Tyso opened wide his dark eyes in astonishment. Mr Mellows, a gaujo, used the word vardo and now he knew the gypsy name for a camping site. Would wonders never cease during this extraordinary week!

The farmer continued, apparently unaware that his language had caused his companion any surprise. "This lad and his mate were sent to move the gypsies on, see . . . They did all the usual things, you know; they told the people to get moving, called them a few names, upset a pot of food

* camping place /stopping place   49

'accidentally'. But they kept asking to stay a little longer. They went on about a woman who was near her time and couldn't be moved. These two lads had their job to do and they wouldn't give way. It was almost dark when the gypsies began to pack up their vardos, for they were travelling in vardos. It was then that a girl, a beautiful girl, came out of the shadows into the firelight. She stood in front of the two gaujos in uniform and cursed them. From what she said they gathered that her sister was in danger and couldn't travel. They ordered the rest of the group to move on but they let the girl stay behind to look after her sister in the tent that, in the old way, had been set aside for her with its mat of plaited straw for the baby to be born onto in the Romany fashion.

One of the lads went back the next day to make sure that the orders had been obeyed. They had. Only the girl was there, sitting beside her dead sister with the lifeless baby in her arms. The upshot of all this was the young copper and the girl got to see quite a lot of each other, what with arranging the funeral and everything, and, I know it sounds strange, within a few months they were married. That didn't do his promotion prospects much good, I can tell you!

When the man's father died the fellow retired from the force in order to manage the family farm. It was to the farm that the girl's father came, trundling his vardo into the yard only days before he died. She's dead too now, of course, but the vardo's still there.''

"Then,'' Tyso gasped as the truth dawned upon him at last, "it was you, you were the copper.''

"Yup. Pass me that roll of barbed wire. Careful. Nasty stuff. You can do yourself a lot of harm with barbed wire. We'll just finish off what's left on that one, and then I'll start on the next roll another day when we have some time to spare for the job.''

Tyso was trying to take in the story that he'd heard.

"The vardo,'' he went on, clinging in his confusion to the one thing that he really understood, "you didn't burn it?''

"No. Seemed better not to. Folks round here can be a bit unfriendly and no one knew that he was here, let alone that he was a relative. No, we had him buried without any fuss, and no one the wiser. There were the children to consider, you see."

"What's wrong with being a gypsy," Tyso growled.

"Nothing. What is wrong is being a gypsy, or half a gypsy, in a world that fears anything that it doesn't fully understand."

"I'm a gypsy." Tyso spat it out defiantly.

"Of course you are, and right now your main interest seems to be the vardo. Why?"

It was no good. He would have to come right out with it. "I want it." There, he'd said it.

Mr Mellows went on steadily doing the fencing. Was there no shaking the man? "Oh yes? What do you want it for?"

"I. . . . Well, I want to do it up properly, and then, when it's all mended and new, I want to take it up north and find my sister and little brother and Gran and take them away with me." The words tumbled out. He felt soft, standing there telling his dreams, but it had to be done.

"Well. . . ."

"I'll find a way to pay for it. I should have a bit of money soon."

"Take a while on what you earn here, even if I only charge you a few quid. It will cost . . . all those materials."

"I know, but I reckon to have more than my wages in a few days . . . possibly a hundred pounds more. Enough to pay for everything, buying price and all."

Mr Mellows didn't look up, but he paused and, though Tyso couldn't see it, an anxious expression came over his face. However, there was no sign of anxiety in his voice when he said, "It's stood there for so many years uncared for that I expect it is pretty rotten. Still, if you are set on having it, I see no reason why you shouldn't. Tell you what, you can have it in exchange for some baby-sitting. Aileen likes to go out and it's good for her, especially on a Saturday, and if I have a darts match she has to stay at home. Yes, you can have it for some baby-sitting."

Tyso couldn't believe it. That was all. He could have it.

51

Just like that! He tried to gasp his thanks but the words wouldn't come. So he stood dumbly holding out his hand to seal the bargain, his eyes shining, whilst all around them hundreds of miles of lonely fenland vibrated with the coming of spring.

13

During the days that followed Tyso spent every spare minute looking over his vardo. He would stand for an hour at a time, hands in his jeans pockets, planning his repair jobs. He'd told Andy about his purchase and his friend's indifferent, "What do you want that old thing for?" hadn't deterred him at all. Andy dreamed of a thousand pounds worth of Honda, with customised trimmings. How could he be expected to understand what Tyso wanted? Andy's world had been greatly lacking in expensive motor bikes and cars; Tyso's had not. What he wanted was the peace of a vanished past, only, of course, that wasn't quite the way in which he would have put it. Even among his own people he would have been considered an oddity by all but a few. How could this gaujo be expected to understand? He accepted this, and the story that he'd been told he kept to himself.

Saturday morning dawned with clear skies and bright sunlight, the type of morning that promises clouds before dusk. Having given himself a good scrub down under the pump in the yard – Tyso put on his clean shirt and red dikla, carefully washed and ironed by Aileen, and having lain low all morning to avoid questions, wandered off casually towards the farm gate shortly before two o'clock.

Tyso stood fidgeting by the roadside. Would they never come? Had he got the wrong day? Wrong time? Had they already been and not seeing him, driven on to find their boss and report his failure to show up? That could be unbelievably terrible. Tyso went cold at the very thought of it. He need not have worried, though, for after what seemed like hours, but was, in fact, only ten minutes, the elegant black car came along. He slipped into the opened door, and before he had time to appreciate the smooth way it travelled they were turning into a long, rutted drove, leading towards distant farm buildings, in the midst of the fields. Now Tyso began to have second thoughts, but one glance at his companions was enough to make him thrust them aside. There was no going back.

The yard was crowded with men gesticulating and arguing as bundles of notes exchanged hands. Beyond the men were cars parked facing forward towards the continuation of the drove as it disappeared towards the horizon. Obviously the meeting place had been chosen with considerable care.

A small, wiry man in a loud check jacket and matching cloth cap bustled up to them, bushy ginger moustache almost twitching with agitation. "Where you bin? Thought you weren't goin' to show up. Sooner we get this over less chance of us 'avin' visitors. There's a lot a money at stake, Nathan, a lot of lovely money," and he tapped his nose and nodded significantly.

"We're ready any time you like." Nathan Lee replied as he took Tyso's elbow and guided him towards the ring that the men were forming in the middle of the yard.

A hush fell as everyone turned to stare.

"That's not Lewis Heron."

"It's a different chavvo."

"It's a substitute."

These and similar remarks were to be heard on all sides. Tyso could feel the anger crackling round him. At this rate, he might well be lynched before he ever reached the ring. The bodyguards muscled a way through the angry crowd.

"'Ere, Nathan, what's goin' on, then?" asked the wiry ginger man, almost dancing in his rage. "What you bin an' gon' an' don', eh?"

"Easy," Nathan said casually, "we don't want any trouble, do we? No point. Someone might get hurt."

Tyso couldn't help thinking that at the moment there was a good chance that the 'someone' could well be himself. But he need not have worried. Nathan Lee knew exactly what he was doing.

By now they were at the centre of the ring and Nathan Lee was smiling calmly around, greeting friends in the crowd with a jerk of his head or a slight movement of his hands, too insignificant to be called a wave. He was making his point without a word. There were many there who knew better than to try and cross Nathan Lee. The small wiry man was getting the message. He wiped his forehead with a filthy white handkerchief.

Nathan Lee spoke. "Sorry about this substitution but it was that or no fight, and I know that many have come a long way for some sport. I couldn't let you down. That's not Nathan Lee's way. Lewis Heron got himself picked up last night. Brawling. Seems they wanted to talk to him about other things as well. I tried to get him out on bail, but you know how it is?" The murmur in the crowd showed that they knew only too well. "Well, I'd heard of this lad so I tracked him down just in time. If you'd rather cancel, it's up to you."

Tyso listened in amazement. He'd been told that the other chavvo had broken some ribs in a practice bout. However, it was far too late now to worry about the rights and wrongs of it, although he thought that it was more than likely that Lewis Heron was really languishing in a cell, probably on some trumped up charge that his promoter had been clever enough to organise. It didn't bear thinking about, so Tyso didn't think about it. It was better that way.

The men in the yard had no intention of going home without watching a fight, and bets had already been placed. If the odds were now rather more uncertain, that only added to the excitement.

The fight was on as Nathan Lee had always known it would be since his chance sighting at a dance hall of the best bare-fist fighter he'd ever seen. He signalled to Tyso to take off his shirt.

Corners were taken. The fighters were introduced by a tough man with long hair and an untidy moustache who was refereeing the event.

Tyso couldn't help wishing that his legs were a little more

reliable, but it was too late now. Here he was and here he must stay until he'd knocked out his opponent, a large lad, with biceps that reminded Tyso of Popeye.

The lad advanced on him, shoulders hunched, fists raised menacingly. Tyso side-stepped and the blow glanced harmlessly off his right shoulder. He continued to duck and weave and his opponent failed to land a punch. This was going to be easy! Tyso relaxed and began to enjoy himself. Suddenly it was as though some one had butted him in the stomach. He reeled back gasping, staggered and regained his balance. He was furious. That was it! He'd had enough.

The cheers that went up as his opponent fell to the ground senseless, caught by a stinging blow on the jaw, were interrupted by the distant wailing of police sirens.

Someone grabbed Tyso and pulled him into the crowd, while quick hands speedily dragged away the other fighter as he lay, still knocked out. Within seconds everyone was in a car, but not before betting arrangements had been settled. The cars slid away up the drove to the road beyond, and from there to the four corners of the country.

Tyso, flung into the back of the Rolls Royce, with his shirt on his back but still unbuttoned, was not quite clear about what was going on. Indeed, it was not until he had been tipped out on the grass verge near the farm, and the car had sped off into the distance, that he realised that no one had paid him a penny.

14

Tyso staggered into the barn. The motes of dust dancing in the sunbeams that crept through the crevices seemed to mock him as they glided past.

He, he, Tyso Boswell, had allowed himself to be fooled! He hadn't been paid. He rubbed his bruised knuckles and thought about the vardo that needed so much doing to it, and he began to lose sight of the barn because of an unfamiliar mist before his eyes.

He had no idea how long he'd been there, but eventually he noticed that the spring sunlight had gone and that he was cold and hungry. If he wanted to go to the kitchen for a meal he would have to tidy himself or they would be asking awkward questions, and right now the one thing that he could really do without was awkward questions. He felt far too much of a fool.

He went out into the yard. The sky was already growing velvety with evening, and occasional pinpoints of light showed the stars were appearing. Across the yard the kitchen light shone invitingly behind drawn curtains. It was a very peaceful scene in which shadows of buildings and farm machinery merged into tranquil pools of darkness. It soothed him and he stretched like one of the farm cats, pushing up his arms and unclenching his fists as though they were paws. The tension rippled away from him as he eased the muscles back into life. Overhead an owl swooped low in its search for prey, and he watched it pass, drawing satisfaction from its effortless flight. He moved towards the pump.

A hand was clasped across his mouth, his arms wrenched behind his back. Shapes emerged from the pool of shadows. Legs, arms and faces, a blur of teeth and dark, mocking eyes;

the struggle when the prey is caught and writhes, helpless in the claws of a many limbed monster.

The kitchen light shone with a friendly glow, but the curtains remained closed. No one opened the back door. The television flickered as the hero raced away from his attackers, and the family bit their nails as they watched him flee.

Tyso was dragged behind the barn and out to where the new fence was being made, the barbed wire fence.

No one spoke.

Once he managed to set his teeth into the soft flesh of the hand across his mouth and was rewarded with a punishing kick, but otherwise he was quite helpless.

There was enough light for Tyso to see ahead of him to where the roll of barbed wire was waiting to finish the fencing job and, suddenly, with a sense of terror that was like an electric shock to his body, he realised what his captors intended to do.

He had no doubt who they were. He could not recognise them, but he knew why they had come. There were the other fighter's supporters; the losers, the ones who had had to hand over money, who had lost their bets. Now they meant to punish him and the punishment they had planned was too horriible to think about. But think about it he must for it was just about to happen. They were going to wrap him in the barbed wire.

Frantically Tyso struggled to free himself whilst hands tore off his clothes and men began to unroll the spiked fence. His feet slithered in every direction as he tried, desperately tried, to break free, if only to the extent of being able to scream for help. This was now made even more impossible as one of the men tore a sleeve from Tyso's discarded shirt and tied it firmly around his mouth.

Tyso knew the blackness of total despair. There was no escape.

He was dragged towards the awaiting wire which was spread out ready to receive him.

Headlights.

A wailing siren.

A flashing blue light.

The pressure on arms and legs suddenly withdrawn. The wire released to coil back upon itself.

The car raced forward. The attackers fled, merging into the shadows from which they had materialised.

It was over.

Above in the deep blue sky the stars shone. Far out over the fens the owl continued his hunt for something small and defenceless to satisfy his hunger, that in its turn was seeking for something small and defenceless to fill its empty belly and feed its young. It was necessary for survival. The pattern had to be. Behind the barn the gypsy boy lay trembling in the mud whilst the scattered attackers made their secret way back to their hidden cars.

"Are you all right, lad?" asked one of the policemen, staring down at him.

"Can you get up? If so we'd best get you inside," said the other whom Tyso recognised as one of the men that he'd seen outside the pub talking to Mr Mellows. This man fetched a blanket from the patrol car and wrapped it round Tyso's shaking body.

Just then Mr Mellows hurried up. "We thought the siren was on the telly," he said calmly. "What's it all about then? Oh it's you two is it. Come for a crafty cuppa, have you?" Then he caught sight of his farm boy. "Good God! Whatever happened to you, lad?" Without waiting for a reply, he went on, "So you were tied up with that fight, were you? I knew that was on the cards as soon as I spotted Nathan Lee hanging around the area. Then you starting on about all the money you'd soon have. I reported the possibility of a fight, of course."

"That's what we were stopping by to tell you, Bill," one of the policemen said. "You were right. There was a fight, but it was broken up and it was over by the time that our boys got there. But Sonny Jim here was one of the fighters, if my guess is right."

"That'll teach you to keep out of that sort of trouble," Mr Mellows said firmly. "Be thankful that these two came along

59

when they did or by now you'd be running blood like a sieve. Bad enough to be going there to bet, but to fight . . . how daft can you get?"

And that was all the sympathy that he got as he was hustled towards the house, warmth and a hot drink. However no questions were asked, and no further action was taken and, in the circumstances, that was quite a lot to be thankful for.

15

After his narrow escape from the barbed wire. Tyso was glad of the quiet, uneventful days that followed. He mentioned the matter to no one, except Andy. He had an irresistible urge to tell someone.

"You gyppos are all the same," his friend said at last. "None of you can be trusted even when dealing with each other."

"Not true," Tyso snapped, regretting that he had said anything. "It wasn't like that." But in his heart he knew that he lied. Nathan Lee had promised him one hundred pounds, and all that had happened was that his rival's supporters had tried to do him over in a very spectacular fashion.

Andy snorted and went on with his work. He whistled. He was happy. He was nearly always happy nowadays and, for him, it was an unusual feeling. Only one cloud darkened the horizon at the moment and that was how to tell Tyso that he was taking Aileen to the disco on Saturday evening and that, knowing Tyso's ability for getting into fights, he would very much rather that his friend found something else to do. Andy's need to lie low and avoid attracting the attention of the local police grew with every day that passed. He could imagine Aileen's reaction to the information that he was on the run, having escaped from the Magistrates' Court some weeks before. As to what her father would say, he preferred not even to think about it! Tyso was all right, of course. Tyso was, after all, his mate, but why couldn't he keep out of trouble!

"Gyppos!" he muttered under his breath, and seconds later found himself head first in the horse trough.

"Gaujos!" Tyso retorted as he pulled him out again.

Andy, furious though he was, knew better than to hit back.

He stumped angrily away across the yard, shouting over his shoulder once he was at a safe distance, "I'm taking Aileen to the Saturday disco and you keep away, do you hear? I don't want you around, causing trouble and getting into fights, and making a bloody nuisance of yourself."

"All right. Keep your hair on. I'm not going anyway. I'm baby-sitting. Aileen asked me yesterday. You're not the only one she speaks to, you know."

This wasn't quite what Andy had expected and it left him without a suitable answer, which was infuriating. He began to whistle loudly and marched into the house with as much dignity as he could muster.

Apart from this incident, life went on smoothly, and if Tyso disappeared for an hour or so at a time to tidy up his vardo, cleaning away the years of rubbish, scraping away the peeling red, blue and yellow paint, no one was unkind enough to point out the enormity of the task that he had assigned himself.

Saturday came and Aileen spent an age washing and drying her hair, whilst Andy eased himself into his new jeans, wriggling across the attic floor like a demented electric eel, and then arranged his hair to his satisfaction. All the while he listened to the heavy beat of the music in his head, hoped his money wouldn't run out and wished he had a motor bike.

Tyso felt good. He was making it possible for the others to have an evening out. He was beginning to pay something towards his debt over the vardo, as now Mr Mellows could go to his darts match and Andy and Aileen could go dancing. Added to which he would be saving money, and all that by just sitting before the telly. Most satisfactory all round, unless Susan played up, of course, but she never did.

Once everyone had left, Tyso and Susan settled down before the kitchen fire and prepared for a comfortable evening's viewing. Susan was very obliging about television, if she didn't understand what was going on, she would stretch out on the rug and crayon or draw. After a while she usually fell asleep and was left where she was until someone took her upstairs on their way to bed.

Outside the wind rumbled across the fens and broke like

great waves against the isolated farmhouse. Tyso settled back in his chair and thought about the vardo, and how one day he would sit before a blazing yog, and then, when the last embers were dying, climb the steps, shut the door behind him, go to bed and lie there listening to the wind howling beyond his wooden walls. He would keep his eyes open for a witch stone, a stone with a hole through it, to ward off evil spirits, just to be on the safe side.

Something rapped at the window.

Susan was already asleep, curled up like a puppy on the hearthrug.

Tyso stiffened and listened intently.

There it was again. A short, soft rapping on the glass. A branch? There was no bush, let alone a tree. Something blown loose in the wind? What was there that would rap as softly as that?

Gunfire crackled across the screen and Susan stirred uneasily in her sleep.

Tyso stood up. This was stupid. He walked quietly to the window, determined to pull back the blind and look out. His hand went up to the thick curtaining and at once the insistent rapping began again. His hand dropped to his side and he stepped backwards, for this time he had heard something more than the tapping; he had heard his name whispered out there in the blackness, his own name.

"Tyso. Tyso Boswell."

Very carefully, he pulled aside the curtain and found himself staring into the grinning face of Nathan Lee.

Nathan Lee jerked his thumb, indicating that Tyso should come outside.

Tyso didn't move.

The man thrust his hand into a waistcoat pocket and produced a wad of notes, clearly visible in the light from the window. He pointed from the notes to Tyso.

"I'm not fighting for him again, whatever he pretends to offer," Tyso thought to himself, and was about to let the curtain fall back when Nathan Lee raised a finger and wrote on the glass: U.O.I.

Immediately Tyso understood. His world cleared. Andy

63

had been wrong. He left the window and went to the back door. The cold wind tugged at him as he opened it.

"Owed you, chavvo. Sorry about the other business. Heard about it too late to stop it." Nathan Lee was not smiling any more. "We've straightened matters, though. Evened things up, you might say. You'll not be troubled again. All right, are you?"

Tyso nodded and grinned cheerfully. Trust Nathan Lee to sort things out! It was good to know who your friends were.

"I could give you more fights in the north, but I've a feeling you'll not be coming." Nathan Lee, impresario of a sub-culture, had become what he was by knowing his people, and he knew that the chavvo standing before him had other dreams in his eyes than bare knuckles on flesh and heavy purses in his hand. It was a shame. He could have made him rich, even made him heir apparent to his own empire, but it could never be. When small, Nathan had gone dukkerin' with his grandmother, and he knew all the signs. This one would never be rich in worldly terms, but there was something there, something that he could not understand, and yet something that he responded to, like a tune heard long ago and now, though lodged in the mind, beyond recall. He sighed, and thrust the money into the strong brown hand before him.

"Take care of yourself. Perhaps I'll see you around the Midsummer Fair at Cambridge. I'll look out for you, any way. 'Night."

Tyso watched him walk away until the light from the back door ceased to show him. After a few minutes, he heard the soft purr of the car as it nosed out of the yard, and he marvelled at his people's skill in slipping in and out of the gaujo's world.

He shut the back door and went into the kitchen. He sat down at the table and checked his winnings. Now he could begin to rebuild the vardo.

16

"I told you, didn't I?"

Across the green fields drifted the ancient sound of church bells. Tyso and Andy stood looking at the vardo, the one with an expression full of satisfaction, tape measure in hand, as he paused from his labours, the other with his face screwed up with concentration as he wrote down some figures that Tyso had been dictating. The pencil was well chewed and the envelope on which he was writing was tattered and torn. The object of the exercise was plain, however, Tyso was repairing his vardo.

"I told you," he repeated smugly.

"All right, all right, so you've got your money." Andy sometimes wondered why he never won anything, not even an argument.

"I've asked Mr Mellows," Tyso went on. "He's going to take me in the car to buy the wood and things I need. He said that he knew . . ." His voice trailed off. It was rare for him to allow his tongue to run away with him, but the excitement of the previous evening, the feel of the crisp notes with their promise of a shining new vardo and a journey away from these flat lands to a reunion with Rosie, Edward and Gran had made him indiscreet.

"Knew what?" Andy asked vaguely, staring at the grubby envelope and hoping that Tyso had said what was written there, but fearing that he had not.

"Oh, nothing."

"You told him about the money?"

"Yup."

Andy decided that, all in all, he'd made a thorough mess of taking down Tyso's instructions. By the look of these figures, all that he would be building would be a rabbit hutch.

Though Tyso could barely read or write, he did have an understanding of numbers, enough to enable him to make basic calculations. He'd know if Andy had written it down wrong.

Mr Mellows strode purposefully towards the boys. "Ah, there you are," he said, catching sight of Tyso. "After dinner I'll take you over to see Noah."

Tyso felt an immense sense of relief. He'd been thrilled when Mr Mellows had suggested recently when they were alone that a gypsy he knew might be able to help. He wondered, though, whether it was something that he could mention to other people.

Glancing across at his friend Tyso saw that Andy had other things on his mind for Aileen had come out to throw some scraps to the hens and he was staring at her lost in some daydream of his own.

Mr Mellows winked broadly at Tyso and wandered off to look at his crops.

After dinner, Mr Mellows, looking slightly pained and feeling very noble, after all he was giving up his Sunday afternoon sleep, set off with Tyso to call on Noah.

Plovers stood stiffly in the fields as they passed, their plumes making them look like Roman centurions on sentry duty. The guardian of the fens, a grey heron, stood among the new reeds by the waterway. A swan glided in to land on the still water and, for a second matched itself upon the surface, perfect in every detail. The harsh fens had woken to the spring and Tyso awoke with them, restless and excited.

Why wasn't his vardo ready? Why did he have to practically rebuild it? The roads were there. Why wasn't he on them? His sturdy grai should be trotting contentedly northwards. His grai! Dear God his grai! How could he ever get together enough money to buy a good grai on top of all his other expenses? After all it would be no use buying a run-down old beast. It would have to be a strong, healthy animal, not from some knacker's yard. Right?

In a field on their left, several horses, one with a tiny foal, were enjoying the unexpected warmth of the sun.

For a moment, a sly smile flickered across Tyso's dark, handsome face. There was a way. The sun went in behind a cloud and he dismissed the idea as stupid. If he stole a horse, someone would catch up with him and then he would have a whole load of new troubles to cope with. Besides, and he couldn't quite explain this even to himself, it would feel wrong to have his beautiful new vardo pulled by a stolen grai. No, it wouldn't do.

The village was typical of the fens. It was grey, unromantic and rather poor in appearance. They drove down the one, colourless street until they came to half a dozen new bungalows set in pairs around an untidy piece of grass.

"Sheltered housing," Mr Mellows said. He stopped the car. "Old people, you know, live here with a warden to keep an eye on them, to see they are all right. You know the sort of thing."

Tyso didn't, but he saw no point in showing his ignorance. In his world the old stayed with their families, either in the same trailer, or else in a separate one near by. They weren't farmed out for other people to look after. Really, these gaujos! Had they no idea of what was right?

They left the car and walked over to one of the buildings.

Mr Mellows knocked.

There was no reply.

He knocked again.

"No use you doin' that," a trim little old lady called out from the window of the next bungalow. "He won't hear you. He'll be out the back. Potters or sits in that bit o' garden of his all the hours of daylight, he does. I wonder he hasn't caught his death a dozen times over, I really do. You'll have to go round the side and through the gate in the hedge." So saying, she shut the window, her duty done, and in order to be able to go into her kitchen from which she had an excellent view of her neighbour's garden. After all what were neighbours for?

Having done as they were instructed, they found themselves in a tiny garden full of daffodils; at least that was the first impression that they gained. Then they saw that it also contained a pocket handkerchief of a lawn, a minute pond,

67

and, hard by the door, an old armchair in which someone sat gazing at them as calmly as if it was high summer. A broad leather belt held up a shabby pair of corduroy trousers. Above these was an old flannel shirt without a collar and open almost to the waist. Then came a cheerful green dikla, and above that was a wizened, nut brown face enlived by the sharpest pair of black eyes that Tyso had ever seen. He didn't have to be told that this was the man that Mr Mellows had brought him to meet; the man who knew about vardos. Who else could it be but one of his own people?

Tyso knew that everything was going to be all right. Even the grai no longer seemed to be a problem.

17

"Hello Noah," Mr Mellows called out. "How you keeping, then?"

"Fair to middlin'," replied the old man, not moving but fixing his eyes on the boy accompanying his old friend. "Fair to middlin'."

"I've brought someone to see you. A young chavvo who wants to know about vardos. He's got one, you see, that he's going to do up. He wants to take it on the road."

"Oh, he has, has he?"

"I thought that, mebbe, you'd be ready to give him some advice. After all, no one knows as much about vardos as you do."

Noah inclined his head slightly to acknowledge the compliment. It was true. He did know everything that there was to know about vardos and there weren't many left you could say that about.

"Good afternoon," Tyso said politely. "I'm Tyso, Tyso Boswell." On this occasion there was no need for any qualms about giving his name.

"Are you now? A Boswell, eh. Well, there's a name to conjure with, to be sure. A great family of the road, the Boswells. Many branches of that old tree, of course. I've met up with quite a few of your family over the years; in every corner of England; fine men, many of them, and lovely lassies." The old gypsy sank back into his chair and silence.

So there they all were in the chill afternoon, the farmer and Tyso standing awkwardly in front of the armchair with its tufts of stuffing sticking out white in a dozen places, and Noah eyeing them thoughtfully from its depths, while the neighbour's curtains twitched.

"Turning cold, Noah," Mr Mellows said eventually.

"Could we go inside, do you think, and show young Tyso the models that you make?"

Noah raised his eyebrows, as if to say, "What a weak lot these gaujos are!" He wasn't cold. He often brought his paraffin stove outside in the evening, and he'd sit beside it until well after dark. Once or twice he'd lit a proper yog, but the warden had come along immediately and had made him put it out. A fire risk, she'd said. He snorted to himself. A fire risk! Stupid old woman.

The gypsy got up and led the way indoors. It was quite thirty years since he'd married his dear dead Molly and come to live among the gaujos, and though he had managed to adapt to most of their ways, he always felt the same tugging sadness whenever he came in from the garden to the stuffy, enclosed and imprisoning house.

He went over to the stove and put on the kettle. "You'll take a cup of tea," he said firmly. It was an order, not an invitation. "Sit yourselves down, then."

Tyso wasn't listening. He was too busy staring around in amazement at the room in which he found himself. Everywhere there were vardos. Pictures of vardos decorated the walls; some were photographs, brown and faded now, and some were paintings, crudely executed, but bright and exciting. More wonderful than these, though, were the beautifully made models that stood on every available shelf and table top. Tyso thought that he had never seen anything so wonderful.

"Does it all himself, you know," Mr Mellows said, as if taking some credit for the craftsman's skill. "He used to make the real thing, didn't you, Noah?" he added, raising his voice, as though the old man had gone deaf suddenly.

"They aren't as old as people think," Noah said as he pottered about getting out his best cups and saucers, all roses and gold and fragile. "Travellers used to go in waggons, more like the waggons on the telly in them wild west films, and, of course, it's them trailers now. Only a short time they had the vardos, but they were best. Yes, that's for sure. The vardos were best."

They drank the tea, sweet and strong, and Tyso felt the old pangs of homesickness, for the time when his dad and mum were alive, and all the world was a happy place to be. Sadly he wondered why things had to change, why did people die and life become unsafe?

"So it's a vardo you want, is it?" Noah said at last, wiping his mouth with the back of a knarled, blue-veined hand. "I wonder what vardo that would be?" he added, glancing slyly at Mr Mellows who shrugged and carefully lit his pipe before speaking.

"Well, Noah, it's just rotting away. You see, Tyso," he went on, "Noah here knew my wife's father. The other day I wasn't absolutely accurate when I said that no one knew about his coming to us. Noah knew. Came to see him one day. Offered for the vardo after the old man died. But the wife, she wouldn't sell. She'd been all for burning it, you understand. A great one for tradition, she was. Even though Noah here only wanted to keep it in his back yard – he had a bigger one in those days – she wouldn't hear of it."

Tyso offered up a silent prayer that this wouldn't stop Noah from helping him. However, he need not have worried.

They talked far into the evening while Mr Mellows caught up on his Sunday afternoon sleep. They talked about the various parts and what should be done first, and the cheapest way to go about it, and where not to buy wood, and who might have plenty of nails that they could spare. Then there was a discussion about obtaining paint in exchange for some digging. Noah took a pencil stub from a vase on a crowded shelf and searched about until he found a used brown envelope, and then began drawing plans.

Tyso was growing thoroughly confused by all the advice and instructions that he was receiving. At last Noah settled back in his chair. "Reckon you'll never manage alone, chavvo. Reckon you'll need some help."

"Reckon he will," agreed Mr Mellows, suddenly very much awake.

"Could come over and sleep in your barn," Noah suggested hopefully.

71

"Sorry Noah. Your barn sleeping days are definitely over, whatever you may say," Mr Mellows said firmly. But come and stay up at the farm for a few days. Tyso's bed is never used." Tyso sat, his fingers crossed, hardly daring to hope. He knew so much about metal that he'd assumed that he knew about working with wood as well, and, of course, he didn't. He was a boy of the scrap heaps, not the timber yards and carpenters' shops. Without expert help he could only fail, and failure was unthinkable.

An old clock in the corner ticked loudly, puncturing the silence and making it intolerable. Outside a car drove past and some people could be heard laughing. How could anyone laugh at such a time as this?

Slowly Noah stood up. He eased his back muscles in a way that Tyso found familiar, and knocked out his pipe in the grate. He reached up onto the mantelshelf and drew from behind the wedding photograph of himself and Molly his buff oblong pension book. This he put in his trouser pocket along with a tin of tobacco.

"I'll just fetch my jacket and I'll be with you."

A couple of minutes later Noah was ready for the road.

18

The weeks that followed were among the happiest that Tyso had ever known. Every spare moment was spent repairing the vardo. Noah would sit on an upturned bucket covered with a piece of sacking and he would control operations down to the smallest detail, emphasising a point with an occasional jab of his pipe stem into whatever part of Tyso happened to be nearest. Occasionally, irritated almost beyond endurance by the hopelessness of his young apprentice, he would creak upright and take over a tricky job himself.

When not working on the farm or the vardo, Tyso was out in the village, and sometimes, the town, purchasing whatever he needed. He ignored the catcalls of groups of lads that hung about at various street corners and hoped that he never met a gang of them in a lonely place. After the fight at the disco, he knew the kind of treatment he would receive if they ever had the chance to catch him alone. Sometimes he was able to work and be paid in kind. It was a way of life that he understood. He was content. Nonetheless, he was always wary, always on the watch. The memory of the barbed wire incident was very fresh in his mind.

By mid-June the vardo stood repaired and looking almost as good as new. If, here and there, the woodwork was a little rougher than Noah would have liked, and if, once or twice, the paintwork blistered as the sun scorched it, then Tyso didn't mind; it wasn't perfect, but it was as nearly perfect as he could manage, and, bit by bit, he'd sort out the minor faults.

Noah pocketed his pension book and his tobacco tin and Mr Mellows drove him back to his bungalow in the sheltered housing unit.

All that remained to be done was to furnish the vardo and

find a suitable grai to pull it. Aileen's sewing machine whirred cheerfully as she turned brightly coloured materials into curtains and bed covers. A visit to a second-hand shop in the town and he was almost set up, and with enough money left to buy a grai, at least he thought that he must have for hadn't he been saving his wages as well as spending his winnings with the greatest possible attention to economy?

Tyso put back the lid on the cheerful teapot with its many coloured flowers. Inside, safely hidden from prying eyes, was a bundle of notes.

Outside the vardo the world was silent with approaching night. The day had been very hot and the light breeze was most welcome as it stirred the red and white curtains. Everything shone in the little home. He couldn't afford as much brass as he would have liked, but Mr Mellows had given him a couple of horse brasses and these, with a third that he had bought for himself, decorated the wooden walls. On the shelf, in pride of place, was a glass vase, the glass cut into deep patterns. Red and pink plastic roses stood tall and straight. The vase and the flowers were Tyso's most precious possessions, apart from the vardo itself. They were a vardo warming present from Aileen and Andy.

Tonight, for the first time, Tyso would sleep in the neat little bunk bed, and tomorrow all his friends would join him round the yog and celebrate the completion of his new home.

It was almost unbelievable.

All the work. All the journeys to the village with their risks of confrontation, not to mention the effort of self-will involved in not hitting out when jibes and taunts greeted him. "How's the Wendy House, eh?" News travels quickly in isolated communities. But he had bitten back his anger, swallowed his pride and kept quiet. He'd soon be away, far away and, with luck, Rosie, Edward and Gran would soon be with him once more, as he'd promised to himself.

He wanted to stay in his own home, in his own world, that evening but he had promised that he would baby-sit for Aileen. She had gone to the shops with Andy and planned to spend the evening with him watching Mr Mellows captain the darts team against its greatest rival, a side from Prickwillow.

He sighed, shut the vardo door and went back to the farm house. Before he went across the yard though, he could not resist one last look at his workmanship as it blazed, red, blue and yellow in the setting sun. Life was good. He picked up a stone and flung it as far as he could out across the fields. He felt the joy and power that horses must know when they roll in the meadows at the end of a day's work. Soon he would be free, really free, and able to roam England from end to end. No more gaujos for him. He didn't need them. He, Tyso Boswell, was his own man, right? He wouldn't make the same mistake as Noah and marry some blonde woman from the town. Not him! He whistled as he went inside and shut the door.

He pulled the curtains in the kitchen because the sun was making the television picture look all faded and vague, and it wasn't much good at the best of times. Susan was, as usual at this time, half asleep on the rug. He settled down to watch a war film that was all about the Americans winning the war, but he wasn't quite sure which war, and anyway, he thought that they were not winning it very well, far too much talking and not enough action. At one point it was a little more exciting with a few guns going off and that sort of thing and he turned it down slightly so as not to wake Susan who was by now fast asleep.

After a while he realised that it was now dark outside. The curtains were no longer shielding the screen from the light, or were they? There was a strange flickering effect, rather similar to that of a defective television picture. Tyso stared at the curtains and tried to puzzle it out. After a moment or two he went over to the window and pulled back the curtain, remembering as he did so that other evening not so very long before when Nathan Lee had been outside with the money.

The sky beyond the barn glowed red.

Tyso screamed.

Susan, accustomed to evenings of noise, slept on.

He tore open the back door and raced across the yard, the

acrid smell of his burning vardo biting tauntingly at his nostrils.

By the time he reached the blaze it was already too late, but that did not stop him. He seized the sack from the upturned bucket and struck out at the fire, but it ate up the dry material in an instant. He grabbed the bucket intending to get water from the pump. The holes in it showed how useless it would be. In despair, he took hold of a plank, one that had been left over during the repair work, and he attacked the blaze with it, striking at the sides only to hear the boards splinter as they gave way under the combined force of the blows and the heat.

The fire crackled merrily and Tyso thought that it was the laughter of fiends.

He remembered the cut glass vase with the plastic flowers and, suddenly all that mattered was to rescue them.

He leapt onto a shaft and little tongues of flame curled round his feet. He pressed his bare hands against the hot, smouldering door and it gave inwards, a great sheet of flames poured out, sending him reeling backwards, his face and chest terribly burnt. But he wasn't aware of the pain. All he knew was that his vardo, his dream come true, was burning up before his eyes and there was nothing that he could do. Nothing.

In utter despair he began beating at the fire with his bare hands.

He didn't hear the cries of horror as Andy and Aileen rushed towards the inferno. He wasn't aware of Andy pulling him clear and rolling him on the ground to put out the flames that engulfed him.

He heard nothing of Aileen's sobs or the gasp of horror that Mr Mellows gave as he knelt beside him. In fact he knew nothing for many days to come, and when he did, once more, become aware of the world around him, he still saw it through a sheet of flames and heard it through the crackle of fire. He heard what doctors and nurses said to him but he had no wish to answer.

The loss of his vardo had sent him into a world of his own from which he saw no point in returning.

19

He knew that they came to see him, Andy and Mr Mellows and, eventually, Aileen. He knew that they brought him flowers, but the flowers that he wanted were the red and white plastic ones in the cut glass vase in his vardo.

They told him that Andy had found a crash helmet which had led directly to the boys who had burnt down the vardo. They told him that it had meant Andy going to the police station and that now he was awaiting the hearing of the court case from which he had absconded during the winter. Mr Mellows was paying for a solicitor and it seemed likely that he would get off with a fine, in view of all the circumstances.

Tyso stared ahead, his bandaged hands lifeless in front of him.

One day Andy told him that the police were going to come and talk to him about the fire, and shortly afterwards a couple of plain clothes men came to the ward and produced a notebook and asked questions.

Tyso heard the questions. In his head he knew the answers. They were like pictures on a television screen. The fight at the disco. The jibes whenever he went into the village. The noises on the television. The blaze. The pain. The grief. Oh yes, they were there. Right. They would never go away. But they were pictures, not words. Words were too weak to express all that. What had it got to do with talking? After a while the nurse came and sent away the men who did not come back again.

Summer changed to autumn and Tyso didn't notice. If there was an outdoors any more all he saw of it was the squares of sky through the hospital ward windows. The only sign of the changing seasons that could be seen there was that now there was more grey sky than blue, and that rain more often lashed at the glass.

The day that the rain changed to snow they told Tyso that they were going to operate on him again, in order to try and graft some more skin on to his face. He didn't bother to listen to what they said. Later, he heard them tell him that the operation had been successful.

It was at about this time that he heard Andy telling him that he had been let off with a fine, albeit quite a large one, and that Mr Mellows was lending him the money. Inside himself, deep down inside himself, Tyso sensed a tiny flame of something not strong enough for gladness, but at least awareness.

By the time that Christmas came, he could walk about and use his hands. The fact that they were rather like claws didn't interest him at all. On Christmas Eve the nurses went through the wards carrying lanterns and singing carols, and Tyso looked in the mirror in the bathroom and was, for a moment, curious about the scarred creature that stared back at him. However, someone came to take him back to the ward to listen to the singing, and his interest faded.

On Christmas Day Andy and Aileen came to see him while Mr Mellows stayed downstairs with Susan. They brought him a number of beautifully wrapped parcels which Aileen undid for him. There was a shirt as well as a pair of brand new jeans and an almost new donkey jacket.

"Like them?" Andy asked hopefully.

Tyso touched the donkey jacket with his claw hands.

"How about putting them on and coming home?" Andy said.

"Everything's arranged. You should have come yesterday only the car wouldn't start, so they said that if we liked to come and fetch you you could come today. Isn't it lovely that we can all be together at Christmas," Aileen said encouragingly.

Tyso thought about what had been said and decided that, despite the donkey jacket, it really was altogether too much effort. He shook his head.

"He understood anyway," she whispered to Andy.

"Come on," Andy said awkwardly, "we haven't got all day. Susan's downstairs and she's been on about seeing you ever since yesterday morning. We won't get any peace if you don't come."

Tyso considered the statement with the contempt it deserved; at least if his expression was anything to go by, but as Andy said to Aileen later, "you really couldn't tell anything from the way he looked any more. His face was so . . ." and his voice trailed off.

A brisk nurse who had no time for special concessions to patients, especially those that interfered with hospital arrangements, trotted up officiously. "Now, now, off you two go. I'll get this young man ready and bring him down to the entrance hall. Have you brought a bag for his things? Ah!" She took the plastic carrier bag with obvious distaste. Wretched gypsies were all the same. Owned nothing and spent all their time stealing or messing up other people's hard earned possessions.

Tyso found himself and his plastic carrier bag down in the entrance hall very quickly indeed.

Susan hid behind Aileen and wouldn't look at him.

The Christmas table was beautifully arranged with sprigs of holly and red candles. Mr Mellows lit these before he began carving the enormous turkey.

The flames flickered and danced. Susan, much subdued until now, forgot about Tyso and clapped her hands in delight. He put his hands to his face, and Aileen lent swiftly across the table and blew softly. Mr Mellows looked up and began to speak but changed his mind. Susan clamoured at the injustice but was quietly distracted by a plate piled high with Christmas dinner.

By evening Tyso was extremely tired and he was thankful when he could go up to the attic bedroom and climb into bed. He'd no thoughts now of sleeping in the barn. No thoughts now at all.

Outside the window the flat countryside was empty of life. It was a mirror of his own existence, a void without beginning or end, light or dark, only flames that burnt unceasingly.

"Can I come in, Tyso?" Mr Mellows said, poking his head round the door. "They're drinking mulled cider downstairs. I didn't think that you would want to be left out so I've brought you some." He held out the glass of gently steaming liquid.

Tyso didn't move.

"Come on, lad, I can't hold this all day."

Tyso wriggled into a sitting position and the farmer handed him the glass. Then he sat down on the bed, carefully avoiding the thin legs beneath the blankets. "Now, you must make this your home. We are all very fond of you and we want you to know that you belong with us." He wasn't one for making speeches, and anyway, he had no intention of telling Tyso that the doctors had said that he might well never recover beyond his present state of health. What Mr Mellows was doing, in fact, was offering his young farm hand a refuge for life, a generous offer indeed coming as it did from a struggling farmer with a family of his own to think about. But then Mr Mellows was remembering a dark-haired, dark-eyed girl, and he knew about happiness lost.

"As soon as the weather gets a little better you can start giving a hand around the place again, if you want to. It's up to you when you start doing things. It won't be for a while yet, though. We've got to give Aileen's cooking a chance to build you up a bit first."

Tyso drank the mulled cider. The warm, spicy liquid trickled down his throat. He saw no reason for discussing his future with Mr Mellows or anyone else; after all, he had no future. There was only the glare of flames and the crackle of fire.

After a while Mr Mellows took the empty glass from his hand and covered him with the blankets as he slid down the bed. Then the farmer went out shutting the door behind him, aware for the hundredth time that Tyso was far beyond his help, and wondering if anywhere there was anyone who could understand and help a gypsy boy suffering from third degree burns and a broken heart.

80

20

From atchin' tan to scrap yard, by pick-up truck and jaguar, a news item was slowly making its way northwards. It was the story of a chavvo who had built himself a vardo only to have it burnt down by a gang of gaujos. He'd been badly burnt trying to put out the fire, and now he wasn't speaking or taking an interest in life at all. What was more, he'd once been a bare-fist fighter of no mean ability, and now he would never fight again.

Eventually, in the natural course of things, the news reached the ringside of a fight taking place in a disused barn in Yorkshire. As soon as the fight was over a black Rolls Royce nosed off to the motorway and headed south.

By now the snow had melted and the first timid crocuses were sprinkled in country gardens. The occasional cat basked in a sheltered corner, and there was that sense of suppressed hope in the air that makes sparrows flutter about with pieces of straw in their beaks though the nesting season is yet some way off. But it wasn't just spring restlessness that was bringing Nathan Lee to the lonely fen farm.

All morning Andy had been busy. He felt tired and dirty and was longing to have a wash and sit down to the meal that he knew would be waiting for him at the house. The ginger and white cat named, for some unknown reason, George, rubbed lovingly round his legs. He bent down and stroked it.

"You're a mess of a cat, if ever there was one," he said, smiling at the ginger dots on the otherwise white neck, and the irregular splodges of colour that mingled in varying shades from sandy to dark cinnamon. The cat obviously considered that some sort of compliment had been paid and purred loudly, rolling on the ground, presenting its pure white stomach to be tickled.

Andy obliged. Indeed, he was so busy tickling George that he was quite unaware that someone was crossing the yard towards him until a pair of shoes appeared on the other side of the cat. He straightened up and found himself looking at a man with a swarthy, weather-beaten complexion, dark eyes, and teeth as white as George's fur.

Andy didn't know Nathan Lee, but he knew the gypsies. As a small boy in Cambridge he had regularly slipped through the wire fence at the bottom of his garden and gone onto the common where they lived amidst their rubbish, their elegant trailers gleaming among the broken perambulators and general litter. It wasn't so very different from the home that he left on the other side of the fence, and he played happily until his mother found out. By then any way, he was old enough to know that gypsies were 'no good' and that they and the gaujos hated each other. Then, of course, he knew Tyso, but, in some complicated way that he never bothered to work out, that was quite different. Tyso was, well, Tyso.

"What do you want?" he snapped, if not out of fear, at least out of an inbuilt sense of self-preservation. He had no wish to be wrapped up in barbed wire or thumped. His hands automatically formed themselves into fists. Though he would never have been a match for Tyso in the old days, he was no mean fighter, and could take care of himself; he had had to, after all.

Nathan Lee tugged at the lapels of his smart jacket, grasping them firmly with his fingers and thrusting his thumbs forward with a defiant gesture that was part of the traditional image of a gypsy, despite his elegant clothes. This wasn't surprising considering that his father had been born in a bender tent, and his mother had sold pegs, heather and lace in order to have enough to rear a ragged family of eight chavvies.

"I've heard as how there has been some trouble," he said softly, his voice hovering on the words like the kestrel, tail outspread, preparing to swoop on its prey from the clear sky above them.

82

"Trouble?" Andy stepped back, stumbling over George who was again rubbing round his legs.

"Aye, trouble."

"What do you mean, trouble?" The cold wind of early spring scurried round the barn and flicked at his jacket.

"Tyso Boswell. They are saying that there has been some trouble."

"Ah." Andy sighed with relief. "Tyso."

"Yes. What's it all about?"

"Well, he built this vardo and then it was . . ." and suddenly Andy realised that the danger wasn't over. Supposing this man thought that he had something to do with the burning. He began again. "There had been a bit of bother with some guys from the village. They had it in for Tyso because he beat one of them in a fight. That was what it was all about and, unfortunately, they came and set fire to his vardo, and he was burnt, badly burnt."

"That's what I'd heard. He's bad, they tell me. Is he?" The voice was still soft but not as threatening now, not as far as Andy could make out, anyway.

"Yes, he's still bad," he agreed cautiously. "Can't seem to take an interest in anything. Just sits, you know." Would he know? Would he understand? Had he accepted the fact that he, Andy, had had nothing to do with it?

Nathan Lee nodded. "Yes. His burns?" he asked quietly.

"He's still a mess. I don't think that he will ever look much again, and his hands, you should see his hands. All the flesh seems to have gone. They're like claws. But his hair has grown again."

Andy had forgotten that the man was a gypsy. All he could think about was his friend's terribly damaged body, and mind. "They got them. They got the bastards. Only for the damage to the vardo, though. Judge said they couldn't be blamed for what happened to Tyso. It wasn't their fault that he tried to beat the flames out. Wasn't their fault! What the hell did they expect him to do? Sit and watch?"

Nathan Lee nodded again. However, he was clearly calmer

than Andy. He had seen it all before. It was a part of the pattern. There was no point in wasting energy in raging against it.

"I've come to see him," he said firmly. "Where is he?"

Andy was unsure what to do. Who was this man? Would Tyso want to see him? After all he had hardly spoken since the disaster.

"I'll have to ask him if he wants to see you," he said carefully.

"Tell him that Nathan Lee has come all the way from Yorkshire to see him, and wouldn't do that for many men."

The name meant nothing to Andy but the way in which the message was delivered did. It was the kind of instruction that you did not disobey, not if you valued your front teeth, anyway.

"Will you come up to the house?" he asked, but the gypsy shook his head.

"No. I'll wait here. You tell him to come out here."

"Oh, I don't know as he will. He won't go further than the back door these days."

"You tell him," Nathan Lee spoke firmly, "you tell him just what I've said."

Andy shrugged his shoulders. "I'll do my best."

As he walked across the yard, he looked back over his shoulder. George was rubbing himself affectionately back and forth over Nathan Lee's shoes whilst the gypsy gazed out at the burnt hulk of the vardo.

Whatever will I do if he won't come out to speak to him? Andy wondered.

Indoors Tyso sat in his usual chair, his fingers twisting endlessly together. His eyes stared vacantly, apparently taking in nothing of what was going on around him. They couldn't, for the glare of his blazing vardo blinded him.

"You've got a visitor," Andy said brightly.

No response.

"He says that his name is Nathan Lee, and that he's come all the way from Yorkshire to see you, and that he wouldn't do that for many men."

A flicker of interest passed over Tyso's scarred face, and was gone. Somewhere inside him there was, for a moment, a light that wasn't a flame, but it faded.

"Aren't you going?" Andy asked apprehensively. He didn't fancy going out and saying that Tyso had refused to come.

Tyso gave no sign that he had even heard the question.

They waited. Andy standing uneasily, and Aileen dishing up the meal but as tense as he was. Mr Mellows was still out.

"Come on," Andy said at last when he could bear it no longer, but Tyso shook his head. He didn't feel up to beating his way through the flames, even for Nathan Lee.

The back door opened and a voice said, "Are you coming, Tyso Boswell, or do I have to come in there and drag you out?"

21

What the gypsy man said to the gypsy boy as he stood holding his arm and gazing at the blackened vardo frame, has nothing whatsoever to do with anyone else. If it was harsh, it was harsh with the reality that belongs to all persecuted races, and that has nothing to do with unkindness. All that matters is that the one, perhaps for the only time in his life, called upon that vast pool of inherited wisdom that belongs to his people and used it to rescue the other from the despair into which stupid cruelty had thrust him.

Shortly afterwards, as he walked home from the fields, Mr Mellows was amazed to see Tyso and some strange man wandering around the wrecked vardo, far too intent upon their discussion to notice him. He did not interrupt them.

"He hasn't been out for so long; he'll catch a chill. He didn't even take a jacket," Aileen fussed in the kitchen.

"That won't kill him," Mr Mellows said, settling down to his steak and kidney pie. "There are far worse things than a chill, lass."

Suitably snubbed, Aileen said no more, but she winked at Andy as she put on the kettle to make Tyso a hot drink just as soon as he came in.

Andy felt contented. His world was ambling back into something like normality. He had dreams of his own that had nothing to do with vardos, or motor bikes either, for that matter, and occasionally those dreams did not seem quite so impossible as he usually imagined them to be. He began to whistle.

"Don't whistle at table," Mr Mellows snapped through a mouthful of pie.

Andy shrugged his shoulders. He'd been shouted at all his life, and his employer shouted less than most. Besides he had reasons for keeping in with Mr Mellows, reasons to do with his dreams, only he did wish that the man wouldn't shout at him in front of Aileen.

Tyso walked into the kitchen alone.

"Where's your friend, then?" Mr Mellows enquired. He'd never quite rid himself of a sense of unease when there were strange gypsies about. After all, things happen . . . things might go missing. You never could be sure. Everyone agreed that gypsies were trouble, and there was no smoke without a fire. It annoyed him that he too sometimes thought like that, despite his promise to his wife, his dear dead wife, that he would always be fair to the gypsies, and help them when help was needed. It was this personal dissatisfaction that made his voice sharper than he intended it to be.

"Gone," Tyso replied sitting down at the table.

"What did he want?"

"Heard I'd been poorly. Came down to see me. That's all." There was a pause and then he added, "He saw the vardo and thinks it can be mended. Says I ought to have a go, anyway. No point in it just standing there, is there? Right. I mean, might as well give it a try."

They all stared at him; not only was he talking, he was talking about his vardo. They could hardly believe it.

For a moment or two no one spoke as they stared at Tyso, taking in this remarkable transformation. It was Mr Mellows who broke the silence.

"Well, lad, it's good to hear you planning again." He added gruffly, "Very good. Only . . ." and here he paused, weighing up in his mind whether or not this was the time to pass on some bad news. He decided to take the plunge. No good the boy building up false hopes. He had to know sometime. He cleared his throat. "Only, Noah, well, he's dead. Died whilst you were in hospital."

For a full minute Tyso didn't say a word, while the farmer silently cursed himself for a clumsy fool. Then to his great relief, the gypsy boy's face cracked into a grin.

"That's all right, I think I can do it with a bit of help. You'd help me, wouldn't you, Andy? You see, there are some things

I might find a bit, well, awkward.'' He glanced briefly at his hands, but only briefly. He didn't wait to hear whether Andy was prepared to help him or not, but went on, ''Nathan thinks it wouldn't take that long. I could be away before the end of the summer. He's going to keep an eye out for Rosie, Edward and Gran, then I'll know in which direction to set off to get them.''

''Of course I'll help you,'' Andy said, as soon as he had a chance to speak, ''but I don't know much about that sort of thing.''

''That's all right. I know what to do. Noah taught me all that I need to know. Nathan says that I can always make it better later on, if it isn't quite right the first time, as long as it rolls, that is.'' He smiled, turning his damaged face into a caricature of its own past.

For several minutes Mr Mellows sat lost in thought as Tyso started to eat his meal. He was delighted with this change in Tyso. However, he was a realist. A hard life in the police followed by a hard life on the land had left him with no illusions. Much as he hated to think about it, there was the question of money. Already he was keeping Tyso, and there were his own children to consider. Andy worked for his wages, but Tyso . . . well. The farm barely paid its way. What with one thing and another he couldn't possibly finance repairs to the vardo, and he knew that every thing that the gypsy boy owned had gone up in the fire. Yet how else would Tyso buy the materials, let alone the grai? He thrashed about in his mind for a solution. Perhaps the Vicar could help. There were various church charities, and he knew that many people in the village had been greatly shocked by what had happened. The question was would such an idea of assistance be acceptable to the lad himself? He cleared his throat.

''I'm glad, very glad indeed, that you are interested in your vardo again. We'll help all we can, that goes without saying. I should think the Vicar might have some ideas as to where you could lay your hands on some cash fairly quickly, so you can get on with the job.''

Tyso looked at him blankly. "Cash?"

"Yes, for wood, paint and so on."

"Nathan's taking care of that." The boy pushed back his chair and stood up. "I'd best go out and start clearing it up a bit, while the weather is OK," he said, taking down his donkey jacket from the hook.

"Don't go tiring yourself," Aileen called after him, anxiously. He looked at her as though she were some alien from another, more primitive, planet. "Don't be daft; I'm not going to melt," was all he said, and he strode out into the yard.

"Very good of that man, very good," Mr Mellows said, adding rather reluctantly, "I only hope that there are no strings attached to the money. You can never tell with that lot."

"Oh Dad," Aileen murmured gently, brushing the top of his head softly with her hand, "you know you don't think that, not really."

The farmer remembered dark hair and flashing eyes and all that had made those few years of his life so happy. He turned abruptly to Andy. "You'd better go and give him a hand this afternoon, I'll manage on the farm. He may think that he's quite well now, young fool that he is, but he's going to find out pretty fast that however willing the spirit is, the flesh is very weak. We don't want him getting all depressed again, not when he's started to perk up a bit. I've had enough of his gloom about the place. Cut along now. Don't stand about gawping, boy."

Andy did as he was told.

Tyso was tugging at the charred timbers, hauling them into a pile away from the vardo, but even before Andy reached him the first flush of energy was over.

"The old man's sent me to help you this afternoon," Andy said, uncertain as to how the news would be received.

"Give me a hand with this," Tyso jerked his head at the plank that he was trying to drag along. Andy took hold of one end and realised at once that Mr Mellows had been right.

Tyso was very weak indeed. After a few minutes the gypsy boy stopped working altogether and sat down on a pile of wood.

"I shall do it," he said as he sat there panting. "I shall do it. I shall have to go a bit slow, right, but I shall do it."

Andy didn't know what to say. How could he say that he understood? How could he promise that he would do his share as unobtrusively as possible. . . . that it would still truly be Tyso's vardo? So he sat down, too.

"It's a messy old job, but you know what has to be done. I'll just do what you tell me. You'll have to do the clever bits, though. I wouldn't be any good at those. It was you that old Noah taught. You're the vardo maker. Maybe we ought to get you the bucket, sack and all, like he had."

They laughed together in the yellow March afternoon and agreed that the 'old fellow' had known what he was doing, even if he only sat on a bucket and gave orders. Andy found a bucket and a sack. Thankfully, Tyso sat down on it.

"I reckon that the last vardo was old Noah's. This one will be Tyso's," Andy said, and he went back to piling up the wood.

Tyso realised with an upsurge of joy that there were no flames flickering before his eyes, and that the sounds of the countryside were no longer masked by the crackling of blazing timbers.

22

Now, with every day that passed, Tyso grew stronger and, if the flesh did not grow back on to his hands, at least he learned how to use them with ever increasing skill. Each day he spent a little less time sitting on his upturned bucket and a little more time working on his vardo. However, he had another problem to occupy his mind, a new difficulty to overcome.

Mr Mellows had been right to wonder if there were any strings attached to Nathan Lee's generosity. His visit to the sick boy, a victim of an age-old prejudice, had been genuine. He was concerned for the chavvo. It was not altogether surprising that the message of the burnt vardo should have travelled over the countryside, nor was it remarkable that someone should have paid Tyso a visit. What was surprising, perhaps, was that Nathan Lee should have come himself rather than send someone on his behalf. However, he remembered the boy's fighting skill, the fat pickings from that day, and way above all he remembered his feeling that this particular lad would go far, not in the sense of making money, but in some other way. It was these factors that brought Nathan Lee down from the north, but once there, once he had got Tyso talking and interested again, something else took over, something that had made him the powerful man he was. Even as they had talked about the cost of the repairs, a plan slid into his mind, a plan to make money out of another fight, a plan in which Tyso could help, could earn the much needed cash for materials rather than he, Nathan Lee, having to fork out a bundle of readies without any return on his outlay. That, after all, went very much against the grain.

It was as the Rolls had nosed its way through the narrow streets of Cambridge on the way to the fenland farm to find Tyso, that it had occurred to Nathan Lee that he would be back in the district in under two months' time for the Midsummer Fair. He'd made some remark to this effect to the driver who had volunteered the information that he hoped to attend his niece's wedding at the Fair, and then added, "Her man's down this way already. He's doing the village feasts*. He'll be at the young chavvo's village in about a month." It was no more than conversation, talk to while away the drive, but the words took root in Nathan Lee's mind. He also stored, quite subconsciously, the information that he saw on a poster as they glided through Mr Mellow's village. It stated that the finals of the district darts tournament would take place on the last Saturday in May under the captaincy of A. L. Mellows.

"When did you say the local feast would be?" he asked his driver. Surprised by the question, feasts are very small beer in the calendar of such men as his boss, the man hesitated, did a few rapid mental calculations and replied, "Well, I can't be certain, but . . . yes, I can. My mate is delivering a new trailer to him . . . we were talking about it a week or two back, and I said . . ." He stopped. Nathan Lee's irritation came over like a wave of cigar smoke. "Last weekend in May," he ended lamely.

"All happens down here!" Nathan Lee grunted. "One long succession of excitements." The driver grinned in appreciation at the wit and with relief that the moment of tension had passed. It didn't do to irritate the boss, not even slightly.

All the information that he had absent-mindedly collected came together as he talked to Tyso and the idea that came to him was far too good to ignore. It was a winner.

Tyso hadn't quite told everything about his meeting with Nathan Lee. He had said nothing about the fact that he was committed to helping the man in some way as yet unspecified, and that he was to meet him in a week's time on a footbridge across the fen dyke, known as the Old Level. It flowed on its slow, grey way about a mile from the farm, beside the road which eventually led to the distant coastal marshes, and there petered out into a world of sea lavender and brown peat pools. He would be there. He dare not do otherwise. Besides he'd do

---

* small village fair held originally in villages on the local patron saint's day

anything, well, almost anything, in order to be sure of enough cash to finish his vardo. Nathan Lee had given him some, not much, to get started, and had promised more, much more, in exchange for what he had described as 'some help with a small business matter'.

As Tyso thought about it, he saw again the gypsy man's dark features and swift, easy smile, admired again the strong hands with their well cared for nails, and envied the strength evident in the sinewy arms. It was, however, normal envy and had nothing to do with the contrast brought about by the flames, for when he was with Nathan Lee he forgot all about his own scarred features and weak hands. Nathan Lee made him feel whole again. Nonetheless the immediate future clearly held problems and it was with feelings that were far from light-hearted that he set out on the appointed day to meet his benefactor.

The day was closing in and the road, never busy, was empty of traffic. Tyso had set out early because for him the walk would be quite a challenge. It was the first time that he had walked so far since the fire and he didn't want to arrive late. That would never do. Twice he had to rest and, by the time he reached the footbridge, he was very tired. It made him angry. Being tired was soft. Right. He knew that he wasn't late because the road, like most fen roads, was straight for as far as the eye could see, and there was no car parked anywhere. There was nothing anywhere, not even a tree. The only buildings were a couple of old sheds beside the road, about a quarter of a mile further on. Therefore it came as a surprise to him when he realised that someone was on the bridge already, not Nathan Lee, but one of his men. The man didn't speak to him, that would have been beneath his dignity. Instead he walked over to the opposite bank and disappeared down the steep slope.

Tyso was not sure what to do. Should he follow? Should he stay where he was? He decided on the latter course. Nathan Lee had said he would meet him on the bridge at four o'clock. It was now four o'clock, according to the black digital wrist watch on Tyso's bony wrist. He leaned against the single bar that formed the hand rail and waited, his back to the water. You never knew with Nathan. Nothing moved. The sun was no more than a yellow smudge out on the western sky. Already the day held the mists of night and the dead rushes rustled brown parchment leaves in the wind. It was cold. Later there would be a frost. Tyso dug his hands deeper into his jacket pockets. The sudden flight of a heron did not startle him; he was aware that it was nearby, conscious of its alert presence as it was of his. It lumbered away upstream, its huge grey wings scarcely missing the water on the downward beat, long legs stretched out behind. The boards creaked. Someone was coming.

"Afternoon!" Nathan Lee joined Tyso at the rail, only he looked out over the water. He had no need to think about his back, and anyway he had two men tucked away, one behind the bank and the other in the Rolls hidden in the sheds that Tyso had seen further down the road.

"How's that vardo of yours coming along, then?"

"'Sall right," Tyso grudgingly conceded. It didn't do to be enthusiastic. Made a bit of a fool of himself last time he and Lee met, didn't he. Wasn't himself then. Wouldn't do for the man to think he was that wet.

There was a long pause. Somewhere below them in the reeds the feathery tops of the dried sedge surged forward as a moorhen made its secret way among the tall stems.

"Getting on with it?"

"Yup."

"Good."

Another long pause. Nathan Lee tucked the ends of his blue silk scarf firmly into the front of his coat as the wind made a playful grab at them.

"You'll be needing plenty of cash, as I told you last time. I can let you have enough, more than enough, to get the job done. Of course, I'll need a bit of help in exchange; not much, just one evening's work."

Tyso gulped. One evening's work! That sounded bad. He had no wish to land himself in trouble with the law, and this had all the makings of an illegal action. Burglary? Yes, that's what it must be. What a fool he'd been to get himself mixed up in this!

"You see," Nathan Lee went on, "That last fight, your fight," and here he paused, winked at Tyso and went on, "and what a fight that was! You know, I've never seen a chavvo of your age put up such a great show, not before, nor since. You were the best, laddie." He paused again, just long enough for the compliment to sink in, and continued. "Now, where was I? Oh yes, that last fight. It made me a handy little packet. It wasn't a waste of time, if you follow me. Naturally," he drew out the word, getting its full value, "I'd like to repeat the performance."

Tyso drew back instinctively, putting more space between himself and the fight promoter. "I . . . I can't fight any more," he said defensively, his voice a shade more shrill than he would have wished.

"No, course not. No one would ask you." Then, because he wasn't sure if that was what he should have said, he polished the toe cap of his shiny black right shoe against his left trouser leg. "But," he went on, "I do have this little job for you, as I have said. He took out an elegant leather cigar case, removed a small cigar, bit off one end and reached for his lighter. As he bent over the tiny flame, the light flickered for a moment across his face, and Tyso shuddered involuntarily. If Nathan saw the shudder he ignored it.

"It's like this, Tyso. I'm going to have another fight in this area. I've got the site, I've got the fighter, and now I need you to help make it all happen."

"I'm listening," Tyso said stiffly.

"It'll take place on the last Saturday in May, eight in the evening. The word is already out. The village feast will be here then and should be in full swing by that time. Also, it's the evening of the darts final and that will have started, too. We'll circle the cars, western waggons fashion and use their headlights. No one will bother us."

Tyso stared at the man in horror. An awful thought was in his mind. Did he mean to use the farm? He couldn't. He mustn't.

"Easy. All over in no time, and no one the wiser. What's more young Heron's back with me, and that's something no one knows. I've let them sort of think that maybe I don't have a good fighter lined up."

Tyso went on staring dumbfounded.

"All you have to do, laddie, is empty the farm for an hour. Yes, an hour should do it."

"You mean . . . you really mean . . ." Tyso gasped out.

"To hold the fight at the farm? Yes. Why not? Perfect place. No one is going to suspect an ex-cop now, are they? And he'll be out of the way with a watertight alibi. He'll be captaining the darts team. All you have to do is see to it that that young gaujo takes the girl to the feast, and you take the little lassie."

Nathan Lee was pleased with himself. It was a triumph of planning and he would stash away a small fortune. He hadn't expected the boy to like it. His sort were funny about some things; he'd seen it before; got caught up with a pack of gaujos and started misunderstanding quite straightforward things. It was gaujo law that made bare fist fighting illegal, not gypsy law. He knew it was dangerous, part of him knew it was wrong, but it was life, the way things were and always had been.

"No," Tyso said firmly.

Nathan Lee took out a roll of money. "You won't get far without cash, young Tyso Boswell." He glanced slyly at the boy. "I do hear as your Uncle Jo gives Rosie and Edward a hard time of it. As for your old Gran, they say it's fair breaking her up." He flicked a ringed finger through the crisp notes.

"It's not right. I can't let you do it," Tyso said, but in his mind he was travelling again up to the camp site where Rosie and Edward and Gran were. His fists were strong again and he was beating Uncle Jo as he deserved.

"No fight, no money, no vardo."

"Just an hour?" Tyso said miserably.

"Just an hour."

"Just this once?"

"Yes. That's all." Nathan Lee nodded, and buttoned up his coat. The interview was over. "Except, that is, for one detail. Young Heron will need to be kept out of sight till the match begins. I'll have him dropped by at the farm the night before. You can hide him in that barn of yours. He'll only need food and a bit of drink. No booze, remember." He turned and whistled softly. The man hidden behind the far bank appeared and hurried over the bridge and on to the road. It was his job to signal the waiting car.

"Haven't said I'll do it." Tyso snarled, hoping he sounded far braver than he felt. The man jerked his head slightly, causing the lank, dark hair to sweep his coat collar, a small movement, the kind that shakes off an irritating insect. He said nothing, but very slowly began to put away the roll of money.

It was growing colder with every minute that passed, and the evening would soon be upon them. All across the great flat lands that stretched out in every direction men and creatures were preparing for rest, while others were stirring, preparing for the hunt. The money slid into Nathan Lee's pocket, and Tyso saw Rosie and Edward and Gran slipping away out of reach, too.

"Right. I'll do it, just this once."

Nathan Lee grinned. "Take this for now. Should get you most of what you need, and there will be more afterwards, so long as we are not interrupted." He handed Tyso a bundle of notes, and then sauntered off to his waiting car, leaving the boy to walk home, unsure whether to be miserable about what he had let himself in for or thrilled about the crisp notes in his pocket.

23

Once again the sewing machine whirred as Aileen made bright curtains and covers. Trips were made along the lonely, straight road to the village, and, occasionally, to the distant college cluttered town of Cambridge, or the lazy streets of Ely, dozing in the shade of the massive cathedral. At first these journeys were for nails and timber, paint and varnish, but later the bulging bags were full of pots and pans, and other things necessary for the furnishing of a home.

"That gypsy friend of yours seems pretty open handed, I must say," Mr Mellows commented from time to time. "No strings attached, I hope." He was secretly relieved that someone was funding Tyso's scheme because it saved him from worrying about how he should keep that rather rash promise made so long ago.

For a couple of weeks it had been a matter of clearing wreckage, assessing the damage and making plans. Now that May had blossomed, however, the fenland was once again feeling the gentle warmth of the sun and it was time to begin rebuilding. For Tyso, though, every day brought the fight closer and with it added anxiety. One matter he was certain about and that was that he wanted to stop sleeping indoors. He couldn't think or plan in the house, and besides, he wanted to be sleeping in the barn on the last Saturday in May, what with Heron being there and everything. At this point his thoughts would go back over his talk with Nathan Lee at the bridge and he would ask himself what he could have done to avoid the mess that he was now in. It wasn't that he felt guilty or scared or anything like that. No, it was that he was terrified of being caught, because, if he was, what would happen to his vardo?

"And where precisely do you think you are going?" Mr

Mellows barked as he lowered his paper and glowered at Tyso. The day had been hard, his back ached, and he had been hoping for a restful evening, and here was Tyso sneaking out of the back door with an armful of blankets.

Tyso stopped. "What?" he asked, delaying the inevitable.

"You heard. I said, 'Where do you think you are going?'"

"Oh."

"Well! Where?"

"Out."

"I can see that, can't I," Mr Mellows snapped, wondering, not for the first time, why he had got himself involved with this gypsy boy from nowhere. "I want to know why." He rustled his newspaper angrily and put it down on the table beside him. His back was very troublesome this evening, and that wasn't the only thing that was troublesome, not by a long chalk.

"I'm going to sleep in the barn, aren't I." The answer was given defiantly with Tyso glaring back at the farmer with all the inborn arrogance of his race.

"Oh you are! And who may I ask says so?"

"I'm not a kid. Right." Tyso snarled, dark eyes flashing.

"I don't care if you are as old as the hills. You are not sleeping in the barn."

"Sleep where I like."

"Oh, really!" In the effort to keep his temper he managed to rick his back. "Ouch!"

"Yes, where I like. It's my life. If I want to sleep in the barn . . ." His voice trailed off for the embarrassing reason that he realised that he was close to tears.

"I'll not have it, lad," Mr Mellows said but his voice had softened slightly. "If it's the safety of the vardo that you are worried about, then Andy can sleep out there and guard it. You, well, I don't reckon you are ready to, not just yet."

Up to this point Andy had been congratulating himself on keeping a low profile. It was something that he was quite good at. He was a town boy, born and bred. For him, the countryside happened to be a place where he was earning his living at the present time. He had no wish whatsoever to be a part of it for twenty-four hours a day. Barns, as far as he was concerned, were definitely for rats, mice, cats and gypsy boys. They were not for him.

"I'm fine," Tyso muttered fretfully. "Anyway, whose vardo is it?"

Mr Mellows, leaned forward and placing one hand on his aching back, gently massaged his spine. "That's enough. I've told you and that's all there is to it. No barn for you, not yet, anyway."

"I'm my own man. I'll do what I want." Tyso fumbled for the door handle.

"That's right enough, once your vardo is rolling and you are off on the road. Then you will indeed be your own man, as you put it. At the present time, however, you are living in my house, and you will do as I say, like it or not." He reached forward very gingerly to pick up his cup of tea from the table, had a couple of gulps, replaced the cup in the saucer, and returned to his paper. The conversation was closed.

Andy didn't complain about sleeping in the barn, although he felt that someone should at least have taken the trouble to ask him if he minded. However, there it was. Every evening as the family prepared for bed, he would collect his blankets and walk out across the yard, airgun in hand. If Aileen sometimes walked with him as far as the barn that did not completely make up for nights spent among the scufflings and scratchings of the barn's regular inhabitants.

Meanwhile, up in the attic bedroom, Tyso tossed and turned and despite the windows being flung wide open, he felt shut in and miserable.

Those wide flung windows were responsible for him hearing something one night that caused him to leap from his bed and lean out as far as he could to see what was going on in the murky yard below. He'd heard something. He knew he had heard something, but what? Only the dim outlines of the various buildings were visible, clustered as if for protection around the little farmhouse. Over the fens moaned a low wind. Far away an owl hooted to some distant, but affectionate, mate. He couldn't see the vardo tucked away behind the barn.

Quickly dragging on his shirt and trousers, Tyso slipped downstairs and out of the house, barefoot so as not to disturb the family. Being shoeless meant nothing to him. He had spent a great deal of his life without shoes and the soles of his feet were tough.

The moon shone from a dark cloud's edge and cast a ragged light over the countryside. It showed the vardo standing starkly proud against the vast backdrop of the flat fields. Nothing moved; no sound. Even the owl had ceased his gentle, remote courting.

Tyso stood still, listening. He pressed one hand against the corner of the barn, the edge biting into the thin flesh. His keen hearing picked out the tiny splash of a water rat plopping unceremoniously into a fen drain – but there was no alarm in that.

The moon flickered behind a cloud bank, but a moment later the cloud had passed leaving her floating on an indigo sea of space. He crept to the barn door and pushed it open. "Psst! Wake up! Something's going on!" he hissed.

Andy startled from his sleep, leapt up, swearing heartily. He grabbed his airgun and followed Tyso to the corner of the barn.

"What can you see?" he asked.

"Belt up, I'm listening."

Silence.

A frog gargled a message from a bed of sedge and received a reply from the base of some bullrushes. Then, silence again.

From close to the vardo, among the loose straw lying there, came a scuffling. A swirl of straw twisted upwards and then settled down again.

Tyso tensed himself, ready to leap forward.

Nothing moved. The straw was still again.

Then there came a sinister screeching sound. A suspicion that had erupted into his mind grew into a certainty and bending low, Tyso crossed the open ground between the barn

101

and the vardo and dropped down on the near side of the waggon. Very cautiously, he peered beneath it, and his suspicions were confirmed. There on the far side, haunches drawn up, was George devouring a rat, whilst a few metres away, another cat, some tabby stranger, was watching enviously. Tyso's keen hearing had picked up the noise of some feline scuffle and his anxious mind had translated it into an attack.

"Cats!" he said, half in anger, half in relief.

"Blimey!" Andy could have said a good deal more.

He certainly wanted to do so. "Can I go back to bed now?" he asked pointedly.

Tyso wasn't listening. He was staring at the vardo and puzzling over the problem of the wheels and axles. Noah's vardo had used the original ones, but the fire must have damaged these badly. Up to now Tyso had dodged this issue but, looking under the vardo, he was acutely aware that something needed to be done.

"I wonder . . . I wonder . . ." he mused, "who knows about wheels and axles?"

"Don't ask me?" Andy snarled. "I'm only on guard duty."

"Ah! and one who sleeps too deep," Tyso retorted. "In future, I'm down in the barn nights, whatever the old man says. Right?"

George, his meal completed, sat smugly washing his whiskers, and casting sly glances of triumph at the stranger who, finally defeated, turned tail and slunk off into the night.

"Suits me. I'm going back to bed." Andy returned to the barn.

Tyso hurried after him.

The hay was comfortably reassuring as he snuggled down into it. Daybreak was near and the sparrows in the rafters were already stirring and, as they unruffled from sleep, a few soft grey under feathers floated downwards. Tyso sighed contentedly but, unlike Andy, he did not drift back to sleep. Instead he lay trying to work out the business of the wheels and the axles. Where could he get help?

24

He was beginning to doze when the barn door opened and he heard Mr Mellows' gruff voice. "Come on, Andy. Are you intending to lie there all day? What the . . .!" He had caught sight of Tyso's dark head.

There was nothing for it.

"Morning, Mr Mellows!" he called out brightly.

"I thought that I told you to stay in the house at night." The farmer's voice was low and threatening, like the rumble of summer thunder away on the long, straight fen horizon.

"Yes, I know, but . . ."

"Don't 'but' me, Tyso Boswell."

"No but honest, I'm fit and well now. I really am. I know because of the wheels and axles."

"Wheels and axles! What in the name of heaven have they got to do with it, pray?"

"I've realised what a problem they are. I reckon I've been too poorly to think clearly before." He stood up and shook the hay from his clothing, and ran his hands through his hair, shaking his head as if he were a dog coming ashore.

"Ah! so that means you're better, eh?"

"That's about it. Yup."

Mr Mellows rubbed a thick finger across his forehead. "You beat everything, Tyso. You really do. You believe because you've thought about wheels and axles you are well?"

Tyso nodded. "Yup. I'm well again. So now I can sleep out here again."

His good sense told Mr Mellows that it would be useless to argue, and that by doing so he could do more harm than good.

"All right, then, but Andy stays out here with you. I don't want any more trouble. You should think about all the

103

trouble you've caused sometime, young man. It swarms to you like bees round a honey pot, and I for one don't want any more of it."

Andy wanted to point out that the chance of him preventing further trouble was extremely remote, but realised that he would be ignored and reconciled himself to many more uncomfortable nights in the barn. "After all," as he said to Aileen afterwards, "it can't go on forever, can it?" But sometimes he wondered.

For several days Tyso tussled with the problem of the wheels and axles. He had no knowledge of such things and longed to ask for advice, but since the barn business Mr Mellows had been far from approachable. Indeed, he had ignored Tyso altogether. Then there was the other business on his mind as well. He'd heard no more. Could it be that Nathan Lee had decided to find another site for the fight? If only he would!

"You'll do no good just looking at it. You'll have to do better than that if you want to be away before the summer is over." Mr Mellows said one sunny morning when he came across Tyso sitting on his upturned bucket, chin in hand, staring solemnly before him.

Tyso was so surprised to be spoken to that, for a moment, he could find nothing to say. Then the words came rushing out. "It's the wheels and axles. I don't know what to do about them. I'm stuck."

"That will be a craftsman's job, I reckon," Mr Mellows stood scratching his head so hard that his cap almost fell over his eyes. "There's no way you could do it. But I think I know a man who could. He was blacksmith over Prickwillow way for years. Of course, he's all but retired now, but still lives that way. He might help you. If you can pay, that is, and if the fact that you're a gyppo doesn't stick in his gullet. He's no lover of gyppos, by all accounts." Mr Mellows wasn't as tactful these days. "No harm in going to see him, anyway. Aileen will lend you her bike, I expect. He lives in the High Street. You can't miss it. There's a metalwork fox and hounds acting as a weather vane on a pole in the front garden. If he boots you out, and he may, then I don't know what you do."

"What's his name?"

"Searle. Jo Searle. Don't you take too long about it. There's plenty needs doing this time of year and you seem fit enough to pull your weight," and so saying he strode off into the fields.

Tyso didn't reply. He was rushing across the yard to borrow Aileen's bike. It was a long cycle ride and by the time Prickwillow came in sight he was quite exhausted. He had forgotten how weak his legs still were. When he reached the village he found that the houses were strung out on each side of the raised roadway and that he was, in fact, cycling parallel with the cottage roof tops. Suddenly, ahead of him, and level with the path, Tyso saw a metalwork fox and hounds, apparently suspended in space. He stopped, leaned his bike against a telegraph pole, went down some steps, through a wrought iron gateway, up to the front door and knocked.

"Yes." The voice came from close to his elbow, and Tyso spun round to see an enormous barrel of a man with curly grey hair cut close to his head, and similar curls over the vast expanse of his chest, exposed by his low cut white singlet.

"What do you want? I've no iron scrap or the like, if that's what you're thinking."

Tyso gulped and started to explain, but Jo Searle was having none of it. "Are you going, gyppo, or do I have to set the dog on you?" As if to support his words, a loud, menacing growl came from a shabby kennel by the house and an enormous alsation sprang out, tugging at his chain.

Mr Mellows had said that Jo Searle was the only person he knew who could help with the wheels and axles. Tyso stood his ground.

"Please help me out," he said, as bravely as he could. "Mr Mellows told me to come to see you."

"Ol' Tommy Mellows! Never!" Jo Searle roared.

"Honest!" Tyso held his ground. The man looked puzzled.

Tyso took advantage of this and went on quickly. "He says you know all about cart wheels and axles and that sort of thing. Says you're the very best."

Jo Searle was listening now. He stood in silence whilst Tyso went on to tell him all about his problems with the vardo concluding by saying, "And so you see, I really do need your help. Of course, I'll pay."

The man said nothing for a few moments then threw back his head and laughed. "Ol' Tommy Mellows says I'm the best. Well, so I am. Look here, gyppo, I'll fix those wheels and axles for you, and charge you a fair price."

Tyso could hardly believe his luck. He'd certainly been smart to flatter Jo Searle. He whistled all the way back to the farm and burst into the kitchen still whistling.

"What a racket!" Aileen exclaimed.

"Jo Searle will fix the wheels and axles," Tyso said flinging himself down in a chair.

"Jo Searle at Prickwillow?"

"Yes."

"How on earth did you get him to agree to do that?"

"Just told him your dad thought he was the best."

"I should think that made him laugh," Aileen said smiling.

"It did. Why?"

"'Cos Dad and he are old rivals. He captains the Prickwillow darts team, and they never have a good word for each other about anything."

"That explains it," Tyso laughed.

Now Tyso's days were really busy as he tried to do his share on the farm and help Jo Searle with the wheels and axles, and all the while at the back of his mind was the fight.

It was a wonderful day when the wheels and axles were finished. It was also an alarming day for it was the Friday before the last Saturday in May. The fight was upon him.

25

By the evening Tyso heartily wished he'd never met Nathan
Lee, vardo, Rosie, Edward and Gran or not. He'd been so
busy dealing with repairs that he'd done nothing about being
sure that everyone would be out of the house on Saturday
evening. Now he must start getting down to it, for what
would Nathan Lee do if Tyso didn't play his part? It didn't
bear thinking about. Added to which was the extremely
uncomfortable fact that Leslie Heron would be spending the
night in the barn and Andy was still sleeping there on Mr
Mellows' instructions. He must be got out.

All these and more uncomfortable thoughts were passing
through Tyso's mind as he wandered back across the yard
towards the farmhouse. The midday meal was as good as ever
but Tyso had no appetite for it. He must get Andy out of the
barn.

"I'm quite well now," he announced out of the blue.

"Fascinating!" Andy said, sarcastically.

"No honest, I'm fine."

"Splendid," Mr Mellows said, helping himself to more
bread. "You'll be able to get on with some real work now
then, instead of frittering your time away on that heap of junk
out there," but he was grinning.

"Yes, no, I mean . . . Look I don't need Andy to sleep in
the barn now. I can take care of myself."

Andy looked extremely relieved and shot a hopeful glance
at Mr Mellows.

"Delighted to hear it aren't you, Andy?" Mr Mellows
grinned again, and Andy nodded. "Well then, I reckon you
can sign off from your bodyguard duties. Tyso here can take
care of himself and don't go expecting any thanks from him
'cos you won't get any."

107

Tyso was amazed at the ease with which he had got his own way, and Andy was absolutely delighted. "You won't have me for company tonight, never fear."

With this hurdle out of the way, Tyso felt that he should tackle the next one whilst the going was good. "You and Aileen going to the feast tomorrow night, are you?" he enquired innocently.

"Well, yes. Actually I was going to speak to you about that," Andy had the good grace to blush slightly. "We do want to go, but it's also the finals of the darts tournament. We were sort of wondering whether you would stay home with Susan."

"I want to go to the feast . . . I want to go," Susan chanted.

"You are going. I'll take you in the afternoon," Aileen said and Tyso's heart sank down into his shoes.

"Don't want to go in the afternoon. I like it with the lights," Susan whined.

Tyso seized his opportunity. "I'll take you. We can go down to the village with the others and then we can go off on our own, round the stalls and rides."

Mr Mellows shot Tyso an uneasy glance; every policeman's instinct told him to beware, but the darts match was on his mind and he could do without the added aggravation of who was to stay home with his younger child. "That's a generous offer, Tyso. Say thank you to Tyso, Susan. You'll have a young man taking you to the feast like the grown up young ladies."

Andy wasn't happy. He didn't fancy the idea of Tyso snooping around when he was out with Aileen, but even that would be better than a row about who would baby-sit. He always came out worse over things like that. As for Aileen, she was only too thankful to be able to get out and she simply smiled at Susan and said, "You can wear your new blue dress."

Tyso's peace of mind was short lived for as he went out to have a quick look at his vardo before beginning his afternoon's work a voice hailed him from the barn. There in

108

the shadows was one of Nathan Lee's henchman with a muscular youth who looked in need of a long, hot bath.

"I've brought Heron. You mind you keep him out of sight until tomorrow evening. There's some food in the bag, bread, cheese, fruit, milk that sort of thing, but he should have something hot, if you can fix it, if not never mind. We'll be over just before eight tomorrow evening. You be sure that your lot is well and truly out of the way by then."

Before Tyso could reply, the man had gone, slipping away behind the barn like a summer shadow.

The two boys sized up each other. Tyso decided he didn't like his guest, not at all, and he would have been more than a little surprised to know that Leslie Heron for his part decided that, partially crippled or not, there was no way he was going to tangle in word or deed with the boy in front of him.

"You best keep to the back of the barn. No one comes in here at this time of year, except me at night. What are you going to do all this time?" For Tyso, inaction was an unbearable thought.

"I've got these," and the boy pointed a far from clean hand towards a pile of lurid magazines stacked in a corner, "and this," he added dragging a torch from his pocket. "Oh yes, and this." This last was a transistor with headphones. "I'll be fine."

"I'll try and get you some chips from the village later." Tyso considered that his duties as a host were accomplished for the present and went about his business as calmly as he could.

To everyone's bewilderment, he announced that he fancied fish and chips and if he could borrow Aileen's bike he'd fetch them from the village. As this statement was made as the family sat down to its evening meal he had little chance of being taken up on his offer, but Aileen still thankful that he'd made no difficulties about taking care of Susan on the following evening, said that if he was pining for chips he could certainly borrow her bike; it would just mean that there was more food for everyone else. So Leslie Heron had a hot supper. When it came to bedtime he refused the chance to wash under the pump, so Tyso curled up as far from the fighter as possible as Heron climbed into an expensive sleeping bag.

The fateful Saturday dawned misty and discouraging, and Tyso went over for his breakfast with a heavy heart. Leslie Heron was still asleep, snoring loudly. Tyso ate his breakfast and decided not to try and sneak out some bacon and eggs. There was, he felt sure, ample food in the bulging bags in the barn, but he did have a second mug of tea, and this he took out to his unwelcome guest.

It was a nerve-wracking day. Every minute Tyso felt sure that the boy in the barn was about to be discovered, but by lunchtime his presence was still a secret. Tyso found an excuse to go down to the village for something for the vardo and again Leslie Heron enjoyed a meal of fish and chips.

The day dragged on and Tyso thought that something must be wrong with his wristwatch as the time crept by, and he tried to concentrate on fixing a shutter to the vardo window. It was the early evening that was worst, though. For once, no one seemed in a hurry to go anywhere. Mr Mellows was apparently glued to the newspaper, Aileen disappeared upstairs to get ready and shortly afterwards Andy went to his room and began a most elaborate wash and brush up session. As for Susan, she had dressed a couple of hours early and during the subsequent long wait had decided to dress up a kitten in one of her dolls' frocks and was now absorbed in the game.

There was nothing for it. Tyso had to sit tight and act naturally. The last thing to do was behave in any way that might arouse suspicions. Worse than the waiting, though, was the uncomfortable feeling Tyso had. He was not altogether sure that his great, many times great grandfather, Tyso Boswell, would have been very proud of him. It was one matter to try to rescue Rosie, Edward and Gran by whatever means were necessary and quite another to cheat on your friends, people who had stuck by you for so long and through so much. But what could he do? Nathan Lee had been a

110

friend, too. Without Nathan where would he be? What chance would he have of even finding his family without Nathan keeping an eye on things? He answered the last question for himself. It could be done, but it would take longer. The other questions, however, he couldn't answer. He was trapped between two sets of loyalties: two ways of life.

"Everyone ready?" Mr Mellows bellowed at last, and they all streamed out to the car, Tyso glancing back at the barn and then as they drove away he turned again, half expecting a cavalcade of cars to have materialised out of thin air, but the road was empty. At first he felt a bit of a fool taking a little girl on the rides and round the stalls, but Susan was good company, and having the time of her life, so after a while he found he was enjoying himself. If some of the village lads laughed among themselves they did not dare make anything of it as Tyso was something of a 'no go area' since the fire. It certainly wouldn't do to start up anything in such a public place.

Mr Mellows had insisted that Tyso should take Susan home by nine-thirty and had arranged for the battered village taxi to pick them up. He said that the child would be too tired to walk home by then but the truth of the matter was that he had no wish for her to be walking down an unlit, lonely road where any shadow might hold a gang of lads ready to jump out on the gyppo in their midst. He didn't think that it would happen, not after the fire, but it was impossible to be certain. Andy and Aileen would make their own dreamy way back, whilst he, naturally, would be busy till the pub closed!

It was a great relief for Tyso to find the farm in total darkness and with no sounds other than the usual snuffling of the animals and the stirrings of hay. The taxi had been told to take them right up to the back door and the driver did this, grumbling the while at the mud. Once inside Tyso made them both some hot chocolate and settled down to wait for the others. It was a long wait, but finally Aileen and Andy returned and Tyso felt free to go over to bed in the barn. It was too dark to see much and he resolved to get up early next morning and check out the state of the yard. It was much later

111

that he was woken by Mr Mellows' voice roaring merrily in the yard, singing some half-recalled song from his youth.

At first light Tyso was up and surveying the damage. The yard was churned up by dozens of car tyres but there was no litter, no cigarette ends. Nathan Lee had seen to it that the whole lot had been tidied up. You never knew, he might be able to use the farm again some day.

Very quietly, Tyso went to the byre and drove out the cattle, then over to the pig sty. Soon the pigs and cows were milling about in the muddy yard, surprised at their unexpected freedom. For more than half an hour Tyso herded and shepherded the animals round and round the yard praying that Mr Mellows was still too full of celebratory drink to hear. Then when the half light turned to cold dawn, he rushed inside yelling that someone had let the stock out. By the time it was fully daylight the pens were full once again and there were not enough tyre marks to make anyone suspicious. Exhausted but happy, Tyso had an all over wash under the pump and went singing to breakfast.

26

"Who won?" Tyso asked slyly as he gulped down the strong tea that was an essential part of his breakfast. Mr Mellows didn't answer at first. His head ached and for the moment his memories were all tangled up with chasing stock and slipping over in the mud. After a few minutes, however, he got the words together. "We did. What did you expect?"

"Congratulations. I thought you had," Tyso said, and then added, "It sounded as if you had."

Mr Mellows glared at him. The trouble was that he couldn't quite remember what had happened after he left the pub, and it meant that he couldn't follow up this business about the cattle and pigs. That was bad enough, but he had an uneasy feeling that Tyso knew this and was somehow using it to his advantage. Best let it pass: best say no more.

Now, the fight behind him, Tyso could really begin to think about the time when his vardo would be finished, and he worked at it during every spare moment of daylight.

Not that he had much free time as, now that he was fit again, he had plenty of work to do. He helped with the feeding and cleaning out of the animals, as well as giving a hand with all the many other jobs that always needed doing. Everyone on the farm had to work hard.

At last came the almost unbelievable day when he stood back and surveyed the vardo in all its glory. Admittedly, this time it wasn't quite as elegant as before, but, as a home on wheels, it was strong enough, and inside it was as neat and cosy as could be. If, somewhere down inside himself, Tyso still remembered the cut glass vase and the plastic roses, and if the shelf looked rather bare, he told himself that they were only extras, and had nothing to do with going to find Rosie, Edward and Gran.

It was already mid-June and Tyso's mind was filled with the problem of finding a strong, healthy grai that he could afford. The money that Nathan Lee had given him on the bridge was long gone, and of the man himself there had been no sign, even though he had promised more money once the fight was over.

One evening as they all sat round the table Tyso was too busy worrying about his finances to listen to what was being said, until the word 'fair' caught his ear. Had he been found out? Was all to be revealed? He clenched his hands under the table and waited, looking intently at each speaker in turn. Gradually he dared to relax. They weren't talking about the feast at the end of May, but about the big Midsummer Fair on Midsummer Common in Cambridge.

"Can't I go?" Susan was begging.

"Perhaps we can take the bus over on Saturday," Aileen replied, glancing shyly at Andy. It was all very well Susan wanting to go to the fair. She wanted to go to the fair herself, but she most certainly did not want to go just with Susan. Not that she didn't love her little sister, of course, but . . . .

Andy tipped back his chair a degree or so further than was wise, and almost crashed into the dresser behind him.

"Mind you don't break that chair." Mr Mellows wagged a finger at his farm hand, who was by now covered in confusion.

"Sorry."

"Don't let me have to tell you again, my lad. Downright dangerous, too."

Tyso was not in the least interested in Andy's love life, but he did make a mental note that there was no way he was helping out by taking Susan. Once had been quite enough, besides a plan was shaping up in his mind, shaping up very nicely. A fair, a big one, would be a good place to earn some quick money. Nathan Lee still hadn't paid him, and the cash was running out. Besides, there might be a chance of finding a grai there.

"When is it, the Midsummer Fair?"

"Starts tomorrow. It will be on for a week," Aileen said.

Tyso said no more, but the next day he helped himself to Aileen's bike and cycled into the village. Here he caught the bus that passed through daily on its way to Cambridge. He felt a few qualms about leaving his work on the farm, but told himself that he had far more important things to think about than work, or, for that matter, bicycles.

The bus passed Midsummer Common as it entered Cambridge, and Tyso quickly made his way back to the fairground. Trailers, side shows and rides festooned the ancient common with bright colours. Of course, at this time of day everything was still. Tarpaulins were draped over hoopla stalls, the rides were motionless, the wooden horses with their red, flaring nostrils and staring black eyes, seemingly caught in some kind of spell. The great wheel stood like some derelict relic from the olden days of mining, whilst the helter skelter raised its fairy tale tower with its pink and white roof above shooting galleries and motionless dodgem cars stuck in some eternal traffic jam. All this lifelessness, however, for Tyso spelt familiarity and a sense of coming home. His people had not been fair people but there were the trailers, large and small, the strings of washing, the prams and the tubs of flowers standing bravely before some of the trailer doors. Here were his people; he was among them again. Here, with any luck, he would find, and buy, his grai. Before that could happen, unfortunately, he must earn more money, more than he could earn on the farm, and the sooner the better.

He wandered down the lanes between the trailers, unsure what to do next. After all there was no reason why he should know any of these people. Indeed, it would be far safer if he didn't know any of them, or at any rate if none of them knew him.

"What you hangin' about fer?" growled a burly man who was standing on the steps of a silver and gold trailer along the side of which was emblazoned in letters a metre high, "Don's Dodgems. The Best on the Road".

"I'm looking for some work for the week."

"Oh, you are, eh? Know anything about cars?" The man

jerked a dirty thumb at the sign. "I've lost my lad. Got into some sort of trouble at the last stop. Dare say he'll be back, though, so don't you go thinkin' it's a long term arrangement or anything. Do you know about cars?"

"Oh, yes," Tyso lied. "I know all about cars. My old man used to help a bloke with cars up north. I used to go along from when I was so high," and he waved a hand briefly at about knee level.

"I'll take yer on fer the week. Collect the fares and break up the jams. Sleep with the show at night to guard it, and clean it up in the morning." He went on to say how much he would pay and added, "and if you have sticky fingers when it comes to the takings, I'll knock you from here to next week and then some."

There was a time when such a remark would have made Tyso very angry, so angry, in fact, that he might have well done some 'knocking' himself, but he was growing-up, and he needed that money.

"You're not a pretty sight, are you?" the man went on, peering at Tyso's scars. "The girls won't be bothering you. Some of the car boys are real pestered, they are. Still, it brings in the business, but never mind. Any port in a storm as they say. Just you wait out there till I've finished shaving, and then I'll take you over." He turned to enter the trailer, but stopped. "Name's Wood . . . Arthur Wood. Mr Wood, to you. Yours?"

"Tyso Smith, Mr Wood." Tyso saw no reason for complicating matters by giving his real name. One could never be too careful.

In the course of the day, Tyso did find a minute to ring Aileen. He told her that he would be away for a week, and that he was sorry about her bike. She started to say that her dad wouldn't be too pleased as there was a lot to do at the present time, and anyway, she wanted her bike so where was it? Tyso, however, had hung up before she had scarcely begun; he had things to do.

Before the fair opened, he made himself useful in different parts of the fairground. All the while that he was cleaning the rides and doing other odd jobs, Tyso was listening for talk of grais, but he heard none. Men talked of cars, of deals, of their girls and their families and all the everyday things that people talk about, but of grais there was not a word. In his heart Tyso had known that this would be the case but he carried on listening all the same.

As evening drew on the lights began to shine, etching the rides in colour, marking them out against the darkening sky, drawing towards them crowds that straggled across the common in ever increasing numbers. It was an encroaching tide of fun seekers, eagerly hurrying to be fleeced of their hard-earned money in exchange for an hour or two of illusion. After all, it wasn't much to pay for a glimpse of dreamland. It wasn't the winning that mattered; it was the throwing of balls at goldfish bowls, and the flicking of hoops at gold watches on impossibly large blocks of wood, and, perhaps above all, daring everything on the relatively danger-free octopus, great wheel and dodgem cars. For Tyso, for one incredible week, it was, not just two hours at the fair, but his life, his job.

The cars sped round, sending out blue and yellow sparks from their overhead rods, and music blared forth discordantly and splendidly with the rest of the fairground noises. It was wonderful to be able to leap forward and rescue drivers who had become hopelessly entangled, whilst the thrill of travelling on the running boards as cars raced towards each other, jumping clear, just before the moment of impact, was impossible to describe.

At the end of each evening, the last straggling groups of fairgoers wandered reluctantly away, casting longing glances at the rides and side-shows which, even as they watched, were doused like so many candles and plunged into the darkness of the surrounding night. Tyso would then prepare for bed. He spread out the blanket Mr Wood lent him in the tiny cabin which was the control room of the dodgem stand. Here he curled up like a young fox, eyes closed but ears alert, and slept easily amidst whiffs of stale fish and chips, hot dogs and diesel fuel. It was beautiful. He never heard anything to cause him to stir in his sleep. Each day dawned bright and clear as the early morning chorus of birds, beginning with a scattering of soloists and reaching its climax with the full choir, heralded a new day. He would jump up, rub the sleep from his eyes, and wonder for the hundredth time how he had managed to live among the gaujos for so long without going mad.

On Saturday, coming towards him through the crowd he saw Andy, Aileen and Susan. Susan was obviously very excited as she skipped along clinging to her sister's hand. "Tyso. Tyso," she called as soon as she caught sight of him.

Tyso waved and leapt on to a moving car to collect a late fare. He made this an excuse to perform a few daring leaps among the cars before joining them on the outer step.

"Hello. Want a ride? I can let you on. No questions. Get it?"

This was terrific: he felt like a king. These were his friends. He beamed. They were not his people, but he was prepared to let them be his friends. "Well, how are you all?" And he patted Susan on the head. He was truly magnanimous in his friendship.

The dodgem stopped rotating. "All aboard," he shouted, as the waiting onlookers made a concerted dash for the cars. "Get in, you three. One in the blue; two in the red." He had seized his two favourite cars. Nothing was too good for his friends. But when he turned, they were not there. They had melted back into the surging crowd. For a moment he could not believe it. His friends! The hurt burnt into him. What had he done? His friends! He went back to taking fares, but he didn't feel like leaping on any running boards. Suddenly he was lonely, friendless in a hostile world that he didn't understand.

It was then, through a gap in the encircling crowd, that he saw it; the grai. It was black, it was sturdy, it was perfect.

27

"Can you take over for a moment, Mr Wood?" Tyso asked, poking his head through the little window into the control room. He hurried through the crowd, elbowing his way along when necessary, for it was essential that he should not lose the grai. Finally, he reached the place where he had seen it standing, but it was gone.

He stood staring about him. People brushed past. The whole, many-aged, colourfully dressed mass of fairgoers swayed on its pleasure-seeking way and left him marooned and frustrated.

"Tyso Boswell," a voice said softly at his side. He spun round and found himself staring into the grinning face of one of Nathan Lee's henchmen. "You're wanted."

The man began to move off towards the part of the common where the trailers were parked. Now Tyso knew he would lose the grai for he realised that if Nathan Lee sent for you, you went, want to or not.

Nathan Lee was leaning against the black Rolls Royce. Its gleaming bodywork reminded Tyso how nearly he had found his longed for grai.

"So you are on the fairground, then?" He spoke casually but his eyes never left Tyso's face. He waved away his henchmen and, like some great prince relaxing out of sight of his entourage, immediately settled comfortably on the sweet smelling, warm, sun-dried grass. "Tell me how it's all been going." With a gracious gesture reminiscent of royalty, he patted the grass beside him.

Tyso dropped down and stretched out to his full length, giving himself up to the warmth and the sunlight and the antics of a small ladybird climbing a grass stem. As he watched the tiny creature, he related all that had been done to

119

the vardo, explaining that it was now as complete as he could make it.

Nathan Lee didn't say anything, but he nodded from time to time.

"And now I am working on the cars. It brings in good money, and I am hoping to hear of a grai, a good one." Here he paused. It would hardly be good manners to point out that he thought that he had just spotted the ideal animal and lost it because of Nathan's imperial summons.

"I'm just over this way for a fight. It's coming off in three days' time. I know that you can't, Tyso," and he cast a glance at the thin brown hands playing idly with the grass stem up which the ladybird was still labouring. "Though, by the look of you, you are mending well. However, if you want to watch, I'll have you collected."

Tyso shook his head. "No, thanks all the same."

"Thought not." Nathan Lee stretched himself like a cat that has been dozing in the sun, limb by limb and very slowly. He stood up and shook the wisps of dry grass from his jacket. Then he moved towards the car, and, as if by magic, his two henchmen reappeared.

"Here." The gypsy man turned. "I still owe you something." He handed the boy some notes. "That straightens the books. Good luck, chavvo."

Before Tyso had time to say anything Nathan Lee got into his car.

"Oh by the way," he said, the window sliding down before him, "I saw a very handy looking grai while I was waiting for you. Belongs to . . ." and here he leant forward and spoke to one of the men in the front of the car. "Ah, yes. It belongs to a man called Butcher. Coconuts. Better get after him, Tyso, before the price goes up. Tell him I sent you. Don't forget now. Nathan Lee sent you." A short pause and then he added, "Your brother and sister . . . The family has moved to a place in Lincolnshire, Scunthorpe way. It's called Whiskey Wharf. Don't know it myself. A very small atchin' tan, I should think."

The window snapped shut.

It was the last that Tyso would see of Nathan Lee for a very long while, although their paths would cross from time to time in the future, but Tyso wasn't to know this, and so all that he did was wave and then run as fast as he could to the coconut stall to find the man, Butcher.

When he reached the stall only a girl stood there, an unpleasant girl with many spots and brightly painted lips and fingernails. At first she couldn't be bothered with the scarred boy who kept insisting that he must speak with the boss.

"Nathan Lee sent me to find him," Tyso said at last.

Immediately the girl's attitude changed. Fear slipped like a mask over the spotted creases of her fat features. She went to the back of the booth and called through an opening, "Dad, there's a boy here says Nathan Lee sent him."

Moments later, Butcher appeared. Tyso knew him slightly as he had seen him around the fairground. He was a small ferret of a man with slightly bandy legs and there was about him that special air which surround those who live among horses. Also, he lacked any charm whatsoever.

"Well, what is it? What do you want?"

"Nathan Lee tells me that you have a grai that I might, just might, be interested in." Tyso replied, trying to sound casual and hoping that he was keeping all sounds of enthusiasm out of his voice.

"I may have, and then again, I may not," said Butcher trying in his turn to sound casual.

"Can I see him?"

Butcher jerked his head and Tyso followed him to the back of the booth where he at once saw his grai.

"How much?"

Butcher stated his price.

"You're joking. If I gave you half of that for that broken down old wind bag, I'd be robbing myself. Look at it! Why, it's only fit for the knacker's yard, and I should know. Haven't I worked with horses since I was so high?" and Tyso waved a hand around the region of his kneecap, and without so much as the hint of a blush as he did it. He ran a hand down the horse's legs, sighing and shaking his head and making

121

little whistling noises of disapproval. But Butcher knew about horses and there was no way that he was going to be taken in by this young chavvo who moved his deformed hand so awkwardly, if tenderly, over the grai's shiny black coat.

"Go without. There are plenty of others who know a good thing when they see one, never you fret." Butcher began to walk off as if the matter was closed.

"Nathan Lee is very set on it, for some reason or another," Tyso lied urgently. "Wants it for some one. Left me to buy it for him and take it there. He'll only give you a tenner less as his top price. It's up to you, though. And," he added as he saw Butcher hesitate and turn pale, "you'll have to throw in the harness too, of course."

Fear, well founded, if there had been any truth in Tyso's remarks, gripped Butcher with icy fingers.

"Wants it himself?" the man stammered.

"No, for someone else, I said," Tyso sounded aggressive.

"Ah, well, anything for Nathan Lee, of course. But you tell him he's got himself a bargain."

Tyso did not waste time in further discussion, but carefully counted out the money, praying that he had enough. He had, but only just.

"I'll collect him this evening, after we close. You take care of him, mind."

No more was said. Butcher knew better than take the risk of offending a friend of Nathan Lee.

Tyso ran back to the dodgems, weaving in and out of the crowd like a snake among fen reeds. He couldn't remember ever before being so happy. If only . . . but he thrust the thought of the disappearance of his friends from his mind. He had to plan.

28

Tyso wasted no time in telling Mr Wood that he was quitting. This was fairly well received and Tyso was puzzled until he realised that the word must have got round that he was a friend of Nathan Lee. He was paid off with the addition of only a few curses, and he worked out the evening. He felt that he owed it to his boss, and besides, it was fun.

As soon as the fair shut down, he hurried off through the littered ground with its pools of light and patches of threatening shadow, past the trailers with their squares of light, their smells of cooking, sounds of laughter and argument, crying babies and late night films. He found his grai standing harnessed with the long reins looped securely round a post. He undid them.

"Bye," he called as he passed the coconut shy, but there was no answer from its murky depths where the stands were bare of coconuts, pikes waiting, it seemed, for the heads of victims.

Once clear of the fairground, he mounted and confidently trotted along the road which he believed the bus had travelled when it had brought him to the city. He had a natural instinct for direction and was sure that he would be able to find his way, after all, he'd been shopping in the City on a couple of occasions.

There were plenty of lamps in the still, empty streets, and these shone out brightly, and if the clopping of hooves on tarmac caused a few light sleepers to stir uneasily, none seemed inclined to get up and investigate. Once he saw a police patrol car, its blue light flashing as it parked and dealt with some incident or other, but he took to a side road and waited in the shadows until it drove past and then he resumed his journey. He was reasonably certain there was no law which said you couldn't ride a horse through city streets at night, but he was a gypsy, and if there was one thing he had learned in his life it was that there was one law for the gaujos and one for the gypsies.

The houses ceased. He was out in the countryside, the street lights twinkling in the distance behind him. Ahead the road stretched, a silver ribbon in the moonlight. Tyso began to whistle. He felt a marvellous sense of freedom. He wanted to go on and on, riding through the beautiful star-studded night, the warm smell of the horse beneath him and the cool breeze brushing past him as he rode steadily forward. At length, however, good sense told him that it would be better to rest up till dawn.

He had quite a long way to go and the cloud banks ahead might well soon cloud the moon. If that happened, it would not be wise to ride a black horse over unknown territory. Especially as it was all too easy to fall into a dyke with banks so steep that you would probably never climb out again. So he began to look for somewhere to sleep.

He saw a gate post standing beside the roadway, the gate long since rotted, and beside the post was the remains of a hay stack. It was ideal. He rode up to it, dismounted, tethered the grai, which began to graze contentedly, and without more ado settled himself down beside the stack. The moon was about to disappear behind the cloud bank but in its last glimmer Tyso caught again the dark beauty of the grai. "Midnight; that's your name," he said softly before turning over and going to sleep.

It was noon when Midnight trotted into the farmyard. There was no one about and Tyso felt a pang of disappointment, but then he remembered how Aileen and Andy had looked at him the previous evening, and how they had disappeared. Perhaps, after all, he did not want to see them. Anyway, he knew where they would be; Sunday or not, they would be getting in the hay crop. Wasn't that why he had hurried home, to make up for clearing out at such a busy time? He fed and watered the grai, and set out across the fields. He saw Andy and Aileen hard at work. He half turned to go back. He didn't want to face them. Then, he pulled himself together. He'd not ridden half the night to turn back now.

He didn't say anything but just took his place beside his friends and worked. No one made a remark, only, after a while, Andy grinned at him, and before he had time to realise it, he was sitting in the shade of the hay bailer eating sandwiches and making dandelion chains for Susan, as though he had never been away, except, of course, he had. And Midnight was waiting for him.

The week flew by as they toiled day after day under the hot sun and by Saturday the hay crop was in and Andy and Aileen went off for the day whilst Tyso made the final preparations for his departure. He checked through his small store cupboard and polished up the harness, and checked and re-checked every detail of his home. When he was satisfied that everything was in order, Tyso built a yog before the vardo and waited for the others to return. When they did Aileen gave him the soup and sausages that he had asked her to buy for him, and they all gathered to cook this last meal. The soup boiled over and the sausages were rather black, but it didn't matter. What did matter was that this was 'it'; his last evening with them all.

Moths danced ghostly in the dusk; bats swooped past and out over the open fields; the ever watchful owl winged silently onward.

They didn't say much, these parting friends. There was no need.

The fire died down to a red glow of embers and they all said goodnight, leaving Tyso to sleep in his vardo for the first time.

He kicked out the final sparks from his yog and, with a last glance at the lonely fenland, went in and shut the door. He'd lit his oil lamp earlier and now, its glow greeted him. He stood gazing happily round his home, and then he saw it! There on the shelf was a cut glass vase full of plastic roses. Andy and Aileen had replaced their gift, lost on that awful night that now seemed so long ago. His happiness was complete.

The next day they were all there to see him off. It was a beautiful morning with a cloudless blue sky that drifted into a heat haze on the horizon. The birds were singing and George the cat was already basking in the sun.

As Andy was helping Tyso back Midnight between the shafts, he stopped and looked shyly at his friend.

"Got something to tell you," he mumbled.

"Oh?"

"Yes."

"Well?" Tyso stooped to lift the shafts.

"Aileen and me, well we're getting engaged."

"Oh are you?" Tyso was concentrating on what he was doing.

"Did you hear what I said?" Andy sounded distinctly rattled.

"Yes," and then the news sunk in. Tyso smiled. "Good. Good." He was unsure of the right words. "Will that mean that you won't be able to buy a motor bike?" he asked as the awful thought of the possible loss of a dream crossed his mind.

"That's right. Not for a bit, anyway. I shall one day, though, I expect."

One day! It was beyond Tyso's comprehension. What use was 'one day'? He would never understand these gaujos, not however hard he tried, but then would they ever understand him?

The goodbyes were said and Tyso drove out into the yard. The others gathered at the gate to wave goodbye, and then went on waving until the vardo was no more than a speck on the long, straight road. They were unwilling to go back to the house because each of them felt that this would be the last that they would ever see of Tyso.

29

The days ran into weeks, summer into autumn, as the vardo made its slow progress northwards into Lincolnshire. To begin with, Tyso had pressed on as far as possible every day, only pulling off the road as darkness fell. After a few days, however, he realised that this was asking too much of Midnight, and he slowed down the pace. There were other facts that he had to come to terms with. His money did not go as far as he had imagined it would, and he was soon having to cast about for ways to keep himself fed. Raids on gardens and hen coops supplied some of his needs, but not all. In the past a gypsy boy would have managed very well in the countryside at that time of year, but Tyso's gypsy blood, though it ran eagerly through his veins, was diluted with twentieth-century living. He knew about can openers and cookers, but not about snares and quietly milking cows at dawn. It was, therefore, necessary for him to find odd jobs along the way. The jobs were always small but one way and another he managed. It did mean, though, that he travelled slowly, sometimes resting in one place for a week.

One night he was asleep in a spinney by the roadside when he was wakened by the police thundering on his door, telling him to move on at first light, or else! On another occasion he tried to pull off the road three times in one afternoon only to be moved on each time. It was never certain that he would find a place to camp. Despite these problems he was happy. He was in his vardo and was moving ever nearer to Rosie, Edward and Gran.

The days grew shorter and the nights colder, and it was on a bleak morning when Tyso first saw a sign-post and picked out the letters that spelled Scunthorpe, but there were no signposts showing the way to Whiskey Wharf. It was probably too small for anyone to bother. Tyso realised that he would have to start asking the way. He didn't like the idea of this. It put you in people's power if you had to ask. That's the way he saw it, anyhow.

"Still, it has to be done," he told Midnight, who twitched his ears and gave his head a little shake.

It seemed to Tyso that he asked dozens of people after that, and after a week he was beginning to doubt its existence. Then one day when a watery sun was shining overhead and even a few birds were singing in the hedgerow, he came across a couple of trailers parked in a lay-by, and asked if anyone there had heard of Whiskey Wharf.

"You'll not be wantin' to go there," said one man, "They're a funny lot. Most of us give that atchin' tan a miss. You don't need to go there, chavvo. There are much better places only a few miles away."

None of these travellers had ever seen a vardo before and they were both interested and amused.

"Whatever do you want to creep about in that cramped old thing for?" asked a pretty girl with dark eyes and bad teeth.

Tyso ignored her and questioned the man who knew where Whiskey Wharf was.

"You don't want to go there. You go up North Kesley way; far better."

"I've got to go there. I'm looking for . . . for some people."

The man looked at him for a moment, weighed something in his mind, and risked it. "You wouldn't be that young chavvo who's out to find his brother and sister, would you, the one that Nathan Lee is watching out for?"

Tyso didn't answer at once. He too was cautious. Yet he had to get there. "Yes."

"Name?"

"Tyso. Tyso Boswell."

"I'll put you on the road. You can follow with the car, Harry. I'll go with him in that," and he nodded with distaste towards the vardo.

After a trip of five or six miles down a series of narrow, inter-linked lanes, they reached a crossroad. The man jumped down. "Follow the road to the right. One mile and you'll be there." Relieved to be rid of such old-fashioned transport, he sat down to await his car. Tyso thanked him for his help and set out on the last leg of his journey.

It was early that afternoon when Tyso drove at last into Whiskey Wharf, a dilapidated hamlet of no more than half-a-dozen houses and a broken down pub by the bridge over the river. Whiskey Wharf was not attractive. You felt that any crime could be committed there.

Not far from the river bank, beside some stunted willows, Tyso saw Uncle Jo's trailer, and there was Uncle Jo sitting by the door asleep with his hat tipped over his eyes and an old coat over his shoulders. Of the others there was no sign.

Tyso tied Midnight to a tree and walked up to his uncle.

"Uncle Jo. Wake up. It's me. Tyso."

The man slowly opened his eyes and stared at the scarred boy before him. He knew who it was. He'd heard the young fool had got into trouble with the gaujos. Serve him right, he'd said. Well, it was no good him expecting to whine his way back now that he was a good-for-nothing cripple. He stood up. "Get lost."

"I've come to fetch, Rosie, Edward and Gran,' he said quietly.

"You've what?"

"You heard."

"Get lost."

Their voices brought out the others.

"Tyso," Rosie sobbed with joy and flung her arms around his neck, while Edward stared, thumb in mouth, at this strange creature. Gran smiled her quiet, knowing smile, while Aunt Sarah opened her mouth to say something, shut it like a trap and went back into the trailer. There was no way that she would bring herself to speak to this ungrateful chavvo. No way!

Tyso had an awkward sort of lump in his throat, but he swallowed a couple of times and, his arm still round Rosie said, "We're going away, Uncle Jo. Me and Rosie and Edward and Gran, we're going away. I'm looking after them now. Right."

"You cheeky little brat." Uncle Jo struck out, but Tyso

ducked in time. "Go in, all of you," Uncle Jo ordered. "I'll deal with this useless whelp."

"That's right," Tyso said calmly. "You go in. Put together anything you want to bring. We'll be off in a couple of minutes, so hurry." He looked at Gran and she nodded. "That's right, dearie. That's right," she said, and Tyso knew that she approved of what he was about to do, although how she knew was another matter altogether.

Uncle Jo had picked up a heavy metal bar that lay among the rusty metal scattered over the site, and now he lunged forward. "You ugly devil," he raged. The blow missed and its delivery threw him off balance. It was Tyso's chance. He steadied himself and then let fly a series of blows which, despite his misshapen hands, had behind them so much natural force and accuracy that in no time the man was staggering backwards as he tried to shield his head from the rain of punches. As he swayed backwards he caught his foot in the frame of a rusty bicyle and crashed to the ground. His ankle began to well immediately.

"And don't you come trying to find them," Tyso panted, "'cos I'll give you more of the same." He went to the trailer door and shouted, "Come on, you lot. I'm ready to go."

They were ready, too, for their possessions were very few. As they came out, Tyso could hear Aunt Sarah screaming dreadful abuse at them, but it didn't matter.

Rosie tucked Gran's arm into hers and Edward toddled beside them as they followed Tyso across the atchin' tan to the willows. Only then did they see the vardo and for Gran, in this day of wonders, it was the greatest wonder of all. "Not since I was a tiny girl," she whispered, "not since then."

Tyso helped them climb up, untied Midnight's reins and leapt to his seat. The vardo moved off along the road. He had no idea where it led, but that didn't matter. He'd done it! He'd kept his promise. They were all together at last. He, Tyso Boswell, had kept his promise. He flicked the reins gently on Midnight's glossy back and began to whistle.

Glossary

Romany words used in this book:

atchin' tan	stopping place, camp
chavvo (chavvies)	boy, child (boys, children)
dikla	small neck scarf
gaujo	person who is not a gypsy
grai	horse
vardo	caravan
yog	fire
to dukker	to tell fortunes
to go dukkerin'	to go out fortune telling

Fenland words used in this book:

drain	a drainage ditch without banks
dyke	a drainage canal, or the banks on either side of it, in which the water is often above the level of the surrounding countryside
drove	a track leading from a road to a lonely farm or farm buildings
feast	small fairs held originally in villages on the local patron saint's day. 'Feast' is a shortened version of 'festival'